She wanted him

Susan was surprised at her own admission. *Nick was her hired date!*

Nick lowered his head and kissed her lightly at first, savoring the teasing touch that left them both hungering for more. He pulled her closer, wanting her to feel the desire she aroused in him. But instead of coaxing him to abandon his restraint as he wanted her to do, she struggled to free herself.

"Will this cost me extra?" Susan demanded. "How will you list it on my bill?"

"Hazard pay!" he snapped in frustration.

Anger and passion made Susan reckless. She was as out of character as this night was out of the ordinary. "Tell me, what services do you render?" She ran her hands appraisingly down his shoulders and chest. *Did she dare take what she wanted?*

"Susan," Nick said in a husky voice, "why don't we stop playing games? We both know what we want." Nick kissed Susan again, and she lost all rational thought. His voice whispered softly into her ear, "Let's go inside...."

Maggie Baker is the author of *Love's Sweet Return: The Harlequin Story*, a study of romance publishing. Inspired, Maggie decided to try her hand at romance and her first Temptation novel is *A Man for the Night*. Not surprisingly, Maggie is a professor of sociology at a Midwest university, just like the heroine of *A Man for the Night*. However, Maggie would like to remind her colleagues that this story is fiction!

A Man for the Night

MAGGIE BAKER

Harlequin Books

TORONTO • NEW YORK • LONDON
AMSTERDAM • PARIS • SYDNEY • HAMBURG
STOCKHOLM • ATHENS • TOKYO • MILAN

Published March 1991

ISBN 0-373-25439-3

A MAN FOR THE NIGHT

1

"I HAVE TO FIND a man for the Faculty Club dinner dance,"
Susan declared to Molly as they walked to Susan's house
from the Humboldt College campus late Friday afternoon. The Minnesota Indian Summer sun shone down
on them in golden streams of light, dancing with the
dusty essence of falling leaves.

"Don't you usually just hang out at the dance with
Richard? You haven't cared about a date before this. Why
start now?"

"It's a question of pride."

"Why?" Molly persisted, lagging two steps behind.
"Slow down, will you? I'm built for comfort. I'm not built
for speed."

"Sorry." Susan slowed her pace. "Richard is going with
Michelle Easton, that's why."

"Who's she?"

"She's the blond bombshell he's been pursuing for the
last two weeks." Susan clutched the handle of her briefcase until her knuckles showed white against the skin.
"As chief confidante, I have been privileged to hear the
seduction battle plan every step of the way. Last night he
scored a direct hit when she agreed to go with him."

Molly shot her a curious glance. "We seem to be in a
militant mood today."

"So now Richard will show up," Susan predicted,
"proudly parading Michelle, undoubtedly resplendent
in gold lamé, while I grace the sidelines with the profes-

sors emeritus. Then the next day, he will saunter into my office to laugh about how he thought Louis Hess was going to get whiplash when he did a double-take at Michelle's pouty lips, sooty eyes, and long-legged sexiness and I will have to laugh with him and congratulate him on his conquest."

"You want to tell me what's really going on here?" Molly demanded bluntly.

"What do you mean?" Susan avoided her friend's eyes. "Just a little healthy competition between friends, that's all."

"Susan, don't tell me about healthy competition when you've been describing thermonuclear war. Now, what gives?"

They reached the old wooden frame house Susan had owned for a year. She pushed open the porch door and picked up the mail the letter carrier had shoved through the slot. "The gas and electric bills, an advertisement for miracle fiber boot and glove liners, and a plea for money to save the Tennessee River snail darter. Great," she said as she sorted through her mail. "Do you get all this stuff too? My name must be on a list somewhere."

"Don't change the subject." Molly followed Susan into the house through the dining room to the kitchen.

"You want a glass of wine?" Susan poured two glasses of Chablis from the green jug in the refrigerator and took them over to the wobbly card table that served as her kitchen table. "You've got to promise that you won't breathe a word about this to anyone." Her hazel eyes were serious as she met Molly's gaze. "Not that it's any big secret," she added half to herself, shrugging her slim shoulders. "If even Fred Harrison knows, then the whole campus must know."

"What?"

Susan sat down and considered where to start. How had she gotten herself into this predicament? "When I first came to Humboldt, I was so preoccupied with finishing my dissertation and preparing classes that I didn't have time to socialize. Then my father developed cancer and died." She didn't need to elaborate. Molly had befriended her during those long months when her father lay dying at home and she had driven the four-hour trek home every weekend in the dead of winter to help her mother take care of him.

"How is your mother?"

"She seems to be all right," Susan answered cautiously. Less than a month after her father died, her mother had been rushed to the hospital with angina. She was in the coronary care unit for two weeks before she stabilized and was able to return home. Even though that was a year and a half ago, Susan still kept an anxious eye on her.

"When Mom was out of danger, I turned my attention back to school. My tenure decision was just two years away and I knew it was publish or perish. I started working on *Men and Women at Work*, sent the completed manuscript in to my publisher last April, and promptly fell apart."

"But I didn't notice anything."

"By then, I had gotten good at faking it. You had been such a trooper that I couldn't burden you with any more problems. Besides, what were my problems exactly? My life was finally settling down. Why should I be so depressed and restless?"

"Oh, oh, I know what's coming," Molly said. "As soon as a woman starts feeling that way, she falls in love."

"You should be the sociologist instead of me since you're so good at predicting human behavior," Susan replied dryly.

"So who is he?"

"Can't you guess? Richard."

"Richard!"

"Is that so impossible? Is it so incomprehensible that Richard might find me attractive?" Susan had asked herself that question many times.

"I don't know. I was thinking more along the lines of why you might find Richard attractive."

"Bless you for that," Susan said with a laugh.

"I never thought about the possibility of you and Richard. I assumed that you were good friends, nothing more, nothing less."

"Well, you were right. The operative words turned out to be nothing more. I found that out when I finally worked up the nerve to tell him how I felt on the first day of classes this fall." With her finger, she traced a heart in the condensation on the side of the wineglass, then rubbed it out.

"I grew up reading too many fairy tales," Susan continued ruefully. "Did you ever read the one about the two sisters? One of them is good, the other is selfish and evil. They meet a witch by a well. The good sister offers the old woman a drink, but the bad sister tells her to get the water herself. The witch puts a spell on them so that every time the good sister speaks, roses, diamonds, and rubies fall from her lips and every time the bad sister speaks, vipers and squat toads fall from her lips."

"Nasty."

"When I told Richard I loved him, I wanted words of love to fall from my lips like diamonds and rubies." She paused, absentmindedly twisting a lock of shoulder-length curly brown hair around her finger.

"And instead you got vipers and toads?" Molly prompted.

Susan laughed again despite herself. "Perhaps not as bad as that. I was incredibly awkward and inarticulate, but I finally managed to tell him that I thought I was in love with him."

"And Richard's response?"

"That's the horrible thing—he didn't respond. He didn't say anything for about a minute and then he started talking about student enrollments and proposed changes in the curriculum—as if I hadn't spoken."

"He didn't say anything? I find that difficult to believe."

"So did I. I was so shocked that I went along with him. We parted for the evening discussing computer literacy of all things! So my confession of love, which was supposed to be all beauty, poetry, and passion ended up being a farce." She shook her head, as if to dislodge the painful memory.

"I don't know what to say."

"Obviously, neither did Richard."

Molly winced. "Sorry, worst possible thing I could have said . . . or not said, as the case may be."

"Don't worry about it." Susan patted her friend's hand. "At least his ignoring me cured me of my infatuation almost overnight. I'm not suffering the pangs of unrequited love anymore."

"What's wrong then?"

"Molly, he made me feel like a gray, sexless ghost." Her face paled with emotion. "I went home pinching myself to see if I was real. I stared at myself in the mirror to see whether I was visible to the human eye. He unnerved me.

I've spent the last month pretending that nothing happened. We lunch together as usual. I force myself to laugh at his jokes and I let him hug me as he did before. I refuse to let him know how much he hurt me, but it's been an incredible strain."

"He's a jerk," Molly said with a rude wave of her hand, which nearly upset her wine. "Forget him."

"Believe me, I have told myself that and recited a whole litany of unflattering observations about his person and character to myself every night before I go to sleep, but I wouldn't have fallen in love with him in the first place if he were as bad as all that. Basically, he's a bright, decent man, but he has a double standard when it comes to women. Plain comfortable women you can talk to are friends. That's me. Poor Richard, I probably scared him to death with my unexpected outburst. Beautiful sexy women who make men's heads spin are lovers. That's Michelle. There's not a thing I can do about that."

"You aren't plain," Molly protested. "All you'd have to do is do something dramatic with your hair, get a facial and a manicure, put on some makeup, you know, the kind that makes you look luminous, buy a slinky dress—"

"Molly, will you listen to yourself?" Susan interrupted. "You sound like a slick make-over column in *Cosmopolitan*."

"Sorry. Another woman falls prey to the glamour industry," she admitted sheepishly. Self-consciously Molly patted her graying hair, which was carelessly pulled into a knot at the back of her head. They both looked at her shapeless dress and her short, ragged fingernails and burst into laughter.

"I don't want him if I have to resort to tricks and artificial stimulants," Susan said when she had calmed down to the point of sporadic giggles. "I want a man to love me as I am. Why does that sound so obstinate and hopeless?"

"I don't know. I'm glad I got married when the way to a man's heart was through his stomach," Molly said, mopping her eyes with a shredded tissue she fished out of her purse. "Learning to cook meat and potatoes has got to be easier than learning how to contour your face."

"That's not all, I'm afraid. My tale of woe gets worse."

"Fred Harrison?" Molly remembered.

"He came to visit me in my office last week." All traces of humor vanished from Susan's voice as she recalled the incident. "He hemmed and hawed for twenty minutes before finally coming to the point. He told me that I seemed like a bright young woman and unlike some of his colleagues, who would remain anonymous, he welcomed women faculty with open arms."

"I bet," Molly muttered under her breath.

"'But,' he said, 'you women must learn that there are certain rules of conduct that must be obeyed' and he told me that I was breaking one of the most important rules. That it was his duty to warn me there were some unsavory rumors about me. My stomach hit the floor at that point. You know he's the chair of the Faculty Tenure and Promotions Committee this year, and I'm up for tenure this coming spring. He said that it was common knowledge that I was having an affair with Richard."

"Susan!"

"Pretty ironic, isn't it? And he wanted to warn me that when I came up for tenure, there were certain people who would vote against me on those grounds alone."

"What did you say to him?"

"I said that we were just friends, of course." She drained the contents of her glass as if to wash away the bitter taste in her mouth.

"What are you going to do?"

"Fred said that I should try to establish an existence independent of Richard so that people would stop thinking of me as Richard's mistress and—"

"Richard's mistress! Does anyone talk like that anymore? I swear the man is stuck back in the nineteenth century."

"He means well, I suppose. He told me that I should cultivate the members of FTP, ask them out for lunch, that sort of thing. When I asked him if that wasn't a bit obvious and calculating, he said everybody does it, that it's just smart politics."

"He probably has a point there."

"He told me that I needed to be more visible on campus. Molly, what is going on? First Richard, then Fred Harrison! You know, I have taken everything for granted—my family, my intelligence, my attractiveness." Susan held the stem of her empty glass so tightly that Molly was afraid that it would snap in her hands. "I never doubted that my parents would live forever, that people saw me as a distinct individual and not merely as an extension of some man, and that one day I would fall in love with a man who would love me in return. Now everything is under siege at once."

Molly reached over and gently pried Susan's fingers away from the glass. "Maybe Fred was exaggerating. I've never heard any rumors."

"You're a friend of mine. No one would say anything to you. Besides, you don't socialize with the members of FTP any more than I do."

"When I was up for tenure, the junior faculty used to refer to FTP as the Faculty Torture and Predestination Committee. We were convinced that the tenure decision was based on how well you played racquetball or how well you fit in at the Faculty Club, not teaching evaluations or publishing."

"I don't play racquetball." Susan observed gloomily.

"Then it will have to be the Faculty Club."

"It won't help matters if I go to the Faculty Club dinner dance by myself and Richard makes a grand entrance with Michelle clinging to his arm," Susan pointed out. "Everyone will think he's dumped me." She stopped, a rueful smile tilting the corners of her lips upward. "Well, he has, hasn't he? But they don't know that and image is everything. That's why I have to find a man, a date who will be as impressive in his way as Michelle is in hers—someone better looking than Richard, taller than Richard, smarter than Richard!"

"Where are you going to get a man like that?"

"That's the problem, of course," she said with a sigh. "Want another glass of wine?"

"Sure."

"The problem is," Susan continued as she pulled the wine jug out of the refrigerator, "I don't know a soul outside Humboldt and what I need is a glamorous stranger creating a stir among the Humboldt faculty—a romantic hit man. Do you know anyone suitable?"

"Sorry. Outside of Humboldt, my social circle revolves around the kids. I could give you an extensive list of baby-sitters, den mothers, and pediatricians, but nary an eligible man. In fact, if I had a list of eligible men, I'd be a rich woman. I could sell it to all my single women friends."

"What about Miguel?" Susan asked, referring to Molly's husband. "Would he know anybody?"

"He works at a day-care center. The only people he knows are mothers and half of them are single mothers who would be the first customers in line for my list. How about going to a singles bar and meeting someone there?"

"No thanks, I've read *Looking For Mr. Goodbar!* Besides, I have a sneaking suspicion that being invited to a formal academic social event is not the result most men have in mind when they go to a singles bar." Susan and Molly sipped their wine in silence for a few minutes trying to think of alternatives. "I suppose I could try the personal ads in *The Twin Cities' Reader*," Susan said reluctantly.

"Good idea! I know a woman who had a friend who met her husband through the personals." Molly bent down and started to sort through the pile of newspapers stacked on the floor by the table. "Do you have a copy of the latest *Reader?*"

"It should be there somewhere close to the top of the pile. Have you ever noticed," Susan asked, her serious tone belied by a faint smile, "that all the personal ads success stories are always third hand? A friend of a friend or a distant cousin's widowed mother-in-law found true love and happiness through the personal ads."

"Don't be such a cynic. Here it is!" she exclaimed and straightened up again, her plump face red from the exertion. "Okay, let's see what's in store for you. Here's one:

'Good Buy! Vintage 1954 model with classy chassis, one previous owner. Options: radio playing rock 'n' roll. Fuel requirements: malts and burgers. Favorite road trips: Twins and Vikings games. Sale ends this week. Act now!'

What do you think?"

"Do you seriously believe for one moment that I would have anything in common with a man who describes himself as a used car?"

Together they scanned the columns, their high hopes fading as one ad after another failed to appeal to them until they came to an ad in the lower right-hand column on the last page.

"This is it," Molly pronounced. "Listen to this:

'Attractive 6' male, 46, Ph.D., likes to travel, sail, go to the Guthrie and Orchestra Hall, sip fine wines by the fireplace.'"

"Sounds pretty good, but he is fourteen years older than me," Susan said doubtfully.

"What does his age matter if he's all he says he is? All you need is one date with him, remember?"

"Two dates," Susan amended. "One date at a safe public place to make sure he's presentable and then the Faculty Club dinner dance."

"Wait a minute, there's more to the ad:

'Looking for a cute, petite 18-22-year-old blond female to share in these and other earthly delights.'"

"I'm too old for him!" Susan exclaimed in disgust.

"Maybe you should write an ad of your own," Molly suggested.

"Right, a totally honest ad in contrast to most of these that skirt a fine line between truth and salesmanship.

Overeducated plain Jane on the rebound looking for intellectual hunk to humiliate former infatuation."

Susan shook her head. "It's not going to work. Even if I could write an ad that would attract the kind of man I need, I wouldn't have time to place the ad, receive the letters, and screen the responses in time for the dance."

"If romance is out, how about the commercial alternatives?"

"You mean hire someone? How?"

Molly waggled her fingers. "Let your fingers do the walking."

"The Yellow Pages?"

"Why not?"

Susan got the phone book and flipped open the yellow pages. "What should I look under?"

"Try escort services."

Sure enough, right after environmental testing services and before estate management were dozens of phone numbers listed for Escort Services-Personal. "This is the best idea you've come up with yet," Susan congratulated Molly. "It will be easier this way, strictly a business proposition. Then I can concentrate on playing politics with FTP, not coy sexual games with my date."

"Read out the list."

"Foxy Dolls, Kisses, Lady Love, Ladies Unlimited . . ." Susan's voice trailed off. "I don't know about you but my idea of an escort service does not include outfits called Foxy Dolls."

"Is that the only type of business listed?" Molly peered over her shoulder.

Susan scanned the list again. "There are a few others that aren't so explicit."

"Try one of them. They can't all be prostitution fronts."

Susan downed a half glass of wine for courage and dialed the number of the agency with the least sexual name—Escorts Unlimited.

A soft feminine voice answered the phone. "Escorts Unlimited where the pleasure you seek is limited only by your imagination."

Susan did not feel that this salutation boded well for her quest, but she persevered. "Do you have male escorts?"

"I'm sorry. We don't service women clients."

I'm not in need of servicing, Susan nearly snapped but she reminded herself that she did need an escort and forced herself to be civil. "Do you know of any other agency that does have male escorts?" she asked.

"No, I don't."

"Oh."

The disappointment must have been evident in Susan's voice because after a slight silence, the woman said in a warmer tone, "Look, honey, if it's a man you want, why don't you come here to work? We may not have male escorts but we have a hell of a lot of male clients and we need a new girl."

"No! No, I...I couldn't do it," Susan stammered, mortified by the conversation.

"What couldn't you do? What is she saying?" Molly hissed in her ear.

"That's all right," the girl on the phone replied. "You don't need any experience. We'd train you."

"You mean that if I said yes, I'd have the job? Don't you care what I look like or anything?"

"She's offering you a job?" Molly clutched at her elbow in disbelief.

"It takes all kinds," the girl replied philosophically. "How about it?"

"Thank you, no. I already have a job."

"Well, if you change your mind, give me a call. My name is Tiffany."

"The day isn't a total loss," Susan announced as she hung up the phone. "I'm no closer to finding a man to take me to the Faculty Club dance but at least if I'm denied tenure this spring, I already have another job lined up."

"She did offer you a job!"

"Yes, I had no idea they had such liberal hiring policies."

"By the way," Molly asked as an afterthought, "why did your voice sound so funny when you were talking to her?"

Susan blushed. "I was trying to disguise my voice in case she recognized me."

"Who did you expect it to be?" Molly hooted. "The Humboldt Dean of Women moonlighting?"

"Who knows? A few days ago, I never would have guessed that I would be asking a hooker for a referral! You want a refill?" she asked, heading for the refrigerator. "It's probably just as well that it didn't turn out. I can just see myself turning up at the Faculty Club with a bored young man named Lance clad in tight black leather with chain accessories. I'd introduce him to one of the key members of FTP like Phillip Hunter. 'Lance,' I'd say, 'this is Phillip Hunter, chair of the theater department. His specialty is oral interpretation.' 'Oh, yeah?' Lance would reply, cracking his gum. 'That's my specialty, too.'"

"You're right," Molly said chuckling. "You can't pick a man off the street and expect him to fit into academia. You need someone tailor-made to impress Richard and FTP." An idea struck her just as she tipped her glass back to swallow. Her hand jerked with excitement and she spilled a third of the wine down the front of her ample bosom. "But you don't need to search for a man who is all the things you want him to be!" She sponged at the damp spot with her shredded tissue.

Susan handed her a paper towel. "Why not?"

"All you need is a man who can *pretend* to be all the things you want him to be. You need an actor, not an escort! And there must be thousands of starving actors out there eager for work."

Susan thumbed through the yellow pages once more and finally found what she wanted listed under modeling/talent agencies. She read off the list to Molly.

"The Elizabeth Mason Agency," Molly repeated after she heard the name. "I remember reading an article about them in the *Minneapolis Tribune* a year or so ago. Apparently they are one of the largest and most reputable agencies in the country."

"The Elizabeth Mason Agency it is then," Susan said as she reached for the telephone.

Before she could dial, Molly grabbed the receiver away from her. "Are you crazy? What are you going to tell them? Escorts Unlimited understandably asked no questions, but a legitimate acting agency is going to want to know why you want to hire an actor. You can hardly tell them that you need a date."

Susan groaned and topped off their glasses with more wine. The jug felt noticeably lighter. "I can't bear it. First, I'm ignored by Richard. Then I'm too old for the lecher in the *Reader.* I've been propositioned by a hooker and now you expect me to lie through my teeth to the Elizabeth Mason agency. Is there anything worth this ridiculous mess?"

"Tenure," Molly reminded her. "The look on Richard's face when you walk in the door with a gorgeous man. Now think of a plausible reason for hiring an actor."

"I can't come up with anything."

"Susan," Molly said earnestly, "if you don't come up with something, you will affirm the wisdom of our mothers' and grandmothers' dreaded aphorism: 'If you're so smart, why can't you get a man?' Think, Susan, think!"

Susan thought and gradually an idea took shape until she had a simple, practical plan. Moreover, it had the merit of approximating the truth. She would put her education and academic credentials to work. She practiced it on Molly a few times and then, steeling her nerve, she once again picked up the phone and dialed the number of the talent agency.

"My name is Susan Harkness," she told the receptionist. "I am a professor of sociology at Humboldt College and I need an actor to work as a confederate in an experiment I'm running."

When the receptionist connected her to Elizabeth Mason, Susan explained as formally as possible, hoping to forestall any questions. "I'm a social psychologist and my research has focused on patterns of social interaction in work settings. I'm particularly interested in the friendship groups that emerge out of informal activities such as office parties and softball teams. Other scholars have found that the introduction of new people into these social groups disrupts their work. Humboldt College has some very distinctive social groups that seem to be united by rank, academic discipline, or extracurricular interests. I want to introduce a new person into one of these groups and study their reaction. The Faculty Club is holding a dinner dance next weekend, which would be a perfect opportunity to run a pretest for the more systematic experiment I plan to run later. I have a very clear picture of the man I need to act as a confederate and the role he would have to play. Can you help me?"

"We have hundreds of actors on our books," Elizabeth Mason assured her. "I'm sure we can find some talent to suit you. Since you don't have much time, perhaps you should come down to the agency as soon as possible. You can look through the head books and if you see someone you like, I can arrange an audition. I'm going to be in the office tomorrow morning. Would that be convenient?"

"It's all set," Susan told Molly when she hung up. "I'm going down there tomorrow morning. She leaned back in her chair. "You know, that was amazingly easy," she said, conveniently forgetting that five minutes ago she had been ready to give up. "Maybe my luck has changed and the meeting tomorrow will go as smoothly as the phone call. I'll find the perfect man and the whole campus will sit up and pay attention to Susan Harkness, scholar and femme fatale." She lifted her glass and clinked it with Molly's. "Life is very sweet," she said and downed the wine.

2

BY THE TIME SUSAN WALKED through the doors of the
Elizabeth Mason Agency the next day, she really was
conducting an experiment, only it was not the experiment she had described to Elizabeth Mason. Instead it
was a personal experiment to see if she had the nerve to
follow through on an idea that she realized had been
largely conceived by Chablis. Never in her entire studious life had she acted so out of character.

The talent agency was housed in an old renovated
brick building in downtown St. Paul. Several blocks
northwest of the winding Mississippi River, this area of
the city known as Lowertown was rapidly becoming an
artistic and commercial center. Susan had often come to
eat fettucini at Alfredo's and to shop at the farmers'
market on Saturday morning but she had never taken
particular notice of the agency until now. The quiet
stately exterior of the building was a striking contrast to
the lively scene she discovered when she entered. The
long, narrow room was lined with white corkboard on
which were pinned hundreds of eight-by-ten photos,
posters, and magazine covers featuring the agency's
models. The black-and-white-checked cushioned bench
to the right of the door was stacked with bags of mail,
some of which had already been sorted into piles labeled
Nancy, Gretchen, and Sigrid. Two rows of desks covered with typewriters, phones, and more piles of photos

and papers were staffed by eight young women dressed in casual clothes and chunky earrings.

"Can I help you?" the woman at the front desk asked, her voice raised so she could be heard over the ringing phones.

"I'm here to see Elizabeth Mason."

The woman buzzed the inner office and told Susan to take a seat. As she studied the red carpet, nervously rehearsing what she was going to say, she could hear snippets of the half dozen conversations that were taking place in the room.

"Bart, your script is here. There have been a few changes made."

"I've had some new shots taken."

"Let's see what you've got then. I don't like this one—looks too matronly. You need to sweep your hair up for height. Make it asymmetrical."

"I see you all over the television set these days. You're the new Jim Palmer."

"The poor man's Jim Palmer."

"I haven't forgotten about doing lunch. I'll give you a call when I get back from Portugal."

"Professor Harkness?" Susan looked up to see a slim elegant woman in her early forties. She was wearing a plain olive draped dress with a wide flat gold necklace, the kind of necklace that always reminded Susan of Egyptian pharaohs. "I'm Elizabeth Mason." She led Susan to the back of the room through a set of black enameled doors ornamented with brass Chinese characters. The office was small, dominated by a large wood desk that, like the desks in the outer office, was covered with photos and files. A striking white paper cut mounted on a red background hung on the wall behind the desk. "Your experiment sounds very interesting. I took psychology in college and I remember a bit about small group dynamics but not much, I'm afraid. Perhaps you can explain more about the experiment and what the actor would be doing."

Susan tamed her nervousness with her most scholarly voice. "As I said on the phone, I want to introduce a new person to a specific group of faculty. I want the actor to be everything that academics most admire, so he must be articulate, well-read, informed about current events, witty, with polished good manners. It would help if he was bilingual or if he has traveled extensively. He should be able to talk intelligently about some sport like racquetball without being a jock. Familiarity with the local theaters and orchestras would be a plus." Susan faltered in her rapid recital, aware for the first time of the arrogance of her request.

Elizabeth Mason smiled encouragingly at her, sensing her dismay. "We may not be able to find someone with all of the qualities you want but we will be able to come close and the actor can improvise the rest."

"I had forgotten that," Susan admitted. "But he would have to be very careful because if there is anything academia hates, it's a fraud." She resolutely ignored the nagging voice that told her she was perpetrating the biggest fraud of all. "When I observe the group's reaction to him, I want to see whether they welcome him as one would expect given their values, or whether they are threatened by him."

"I think you also said you had a certain look in mind?"

"He must be fairly tall, six feet or over, and good-looking in a strong, distinctive way. He can't be a pretty boy. He must have character in his face."

"Why don't you start with the look? You can go through the head books that include our clients' pictures

.and information on height, weight, hair and eye color. Pick out anyone you think would fit your description and then I can pull his file and tell you if he does improvisation and whether he is available."

Susan pored over the books. She carefully examined each photo, rejecting this one because she didn't like his nose, that one because he was bald, another one for no reason at all except that she felt like it. She felt powerful; the act of choosing and discarding worked like a soothing balm on her battered ego. Eventually she selected four finalists whom she presented to Elizabeth.

"Scott Brady," Elizabeth mumbled, checking her files. "Oh, yes. He has a lot of improvisation experience. Oops, I see that he has left for Los Angeles to work with an improv group at The Comedy Store. Let's see your next choice."

She worked her way though the list but for one reason or another, none of the actors Susan had picked were available or appropriate. Elizabeth was about to send Susan back to the books to pick some more actors with a less critical eye when she looked at her speculatively. "I wonder."

She went back to her files and pulled one out of the bottom drawer. "I don't keep this one in the books because he is very particular about the jobs he takes, but now that I think of it, he would be perfect for you. He's an excellent actor, a natural talent. He has only done voice-overs and a few industrial films so he won't be as recognizable as Bob Maples," she said, referring to an actor they had ruled out because he had just finished filming a toilet bowl cleanser commercial that was going to be aired every fifteen minutes for the next month on all of the major Twin Cities television stations.

"His name is Nicholas Taurage. He lived in Europe for five years and goes back to visit friends every spring. That would meet one of your requirements. Do you know Roughwood Press?"

Susan nodded. Roughwood was a small local press that had a good reputation for publishing regional poetry, fiction, and literary criticism that was both innovative and true to its roots.

"Nick and Jack Philby own it. Nick maintains he's only a silent partner but that's not true. I know that Jack wouldn't dream of publishing a book without clearing it with Nick. Nick keeps his distance because he doesn't want to be involved in the day-to-day operations of the business. I guess he had enough of that as a young man when he ran his family's clothing store.

"He spends most of his time these days restoring old houses. He buys the most ramshackle wrecks you can imagine and studies the history of the neighborhood and the house before he starts to work on it. He modernizes the plumbing, electricity, and heating, but after that, he is absolutely puritanical about restoring the house to its original beauty. You or I wouldn't think there was any original beauty in some of the houses but he sees it and reveals it, too, by the time he's done. Between his traveling, carpentry and poetry, he's really a modern-day Renaissance man," Elizabeth concluded grandly.

The man must be hideously ugly, Susan thought. Either that or she's in love with him.

"Nick will kill me if he knew I was running on like this, but I've known him ever since he and my brother Eric became best friends in third grade, so I take a proprietary interest in him."

Hideously ugly, Susan decided.

"Here is a picture," Elizabeth said and handed her a color photo. "If you think the look is right, you should consider him."

Susan studied the picture and the statistics. Nicholas Taurage. Height: 6'2" Weight: 196 Hair: Black Eyes: Brown

In graduate school, she had read a book called *How to Lie with Statistics* and here was a perfect example. The statistics didn't mention that his black hair curled seductively over the tip of his ear or that his brown eyes were flecked with gold. Neither did they convey the effect of the faint scar cutting through his right eyebrow before angling rakishly across his temple. How could mere words and numbers describe his firm lips, curved into a slight smile that was half an invitation and half a taunt? To look like this, he must have stared coolly into the camera, as if daring it to steal his soul. He was the most magnificent male she had ever seen.

She casually handed the picture back to Elizabeth. "He'll do," she said.

THE PHONE HAD RUNG five times before Nick, with a barely smothered oath, put down the piece of oak trim he was carving and threaded his way through the sawhorses and canvas floor drops to answer it. The deep scowl furrowing his forehead vanished as he heard Elizabeth's familiar voice.

"I have a job for you," she announced.

"Now that's what I have always liked about you, Lizzie. You waste no time on pleasantries. You just go straight to the heart of the matter rather like a well-aimed sledgehammer."

Elizabeth choked back a snort of laughter. "Very well, Nicholas," she said formally. "We'll do it your way. How are you?"

"I'm fine, thank you. And you?"

"Fine."

"And your charming family?"

"Also fine."

"I do like to observe the social amenities," Nick said with such amiability that Elizabeth knew he was teasing her.

"No, you don't," she retorted. "You're the rudest man I know. Now do you want to hear about the job or not?"

"Yes, ma'am."

"Dr. Harkness, a sociology professor at Humboldt College needs an actor to participate in an experiment."

"Sorry, I'm not interested." Every instinct for self-preservation cried out No!

"Why not?" she asked, clearly astonished at his point-blank refusal. "It's not like you to turn down a role that promises to be out of the ordinary."

"I can't stand the university crowd."

The curt tone of his voice triggered her memory. "Well," she said, steeling her nerve, knowing she was about to risk their friendship, "Pamela Whitbread certainly did a job on you."

Nick expelled his breath in a sudden rush as if she had just punched him in the stomach.

"Nicky?" His silence scared her. She had gone too far. "Nicky, I'm sorry. Please say something. Are you all right?"

The concern in her voice brought him back. "Yes, I'm all right. You just caught me off guard, that's all."

"I'm sorry," she repeated.

"It's not your fault that I was so stupid."

"You don't have to compound your stupidity by avoiding anything that reminds you of her. There are other professors in the world beside Pamela Whitbread. She is not the sum total of academic life." She paused. "Shall I continue the lecture?"

"No," Nick replied softly, smiling as he remembered all the time she had scolded Eric and him with this same maternal affection.

"You're surely not still in love with her, are you?"

"No, of course not. I seldom think of her. It was a knee-jerk reaction, that's all."

"Then why not take the job? It would be good for you. All you have to do is accompany Dr. Harkness to a Faculty Club dinner dance and socialize."

"What kind of experiment is that?"

"She's testing the effect the introduction of a stranger has on an established work group. As I understand it, she wants to see whether the other professors welcome you or feel threatened by you."

"It's more likely I'll feel threatened by them," he commented ruefully. If the truth be told, he was as surprised as Elizabeth at his reaction to the proposed job. He had thought that after all he had gone through and accomplished, he was invulnerable but apparently he was still smarting from the wounds Pamela had inflicted. It was with a certain degree of self-mockery that he recognized that it was his ego that was the injured party, not his heart.

"You'll do fine."

"I don't know if I want to do fine. It sounds like Dr. Harkness is going to deliberately deceive people she works with, people to whom she should have some ties of loyalty, for the sake of her research. She will get published and reap the rewards of her profession. What will they get in return? They'll get exposed to public ridicule." His voice hardened. "I speak from personal experience here."

Not for the first time, Elizabeth mentally consigned Pamela Whitbread to perdition. "Susan Harkness is not an insensitive, manipulative, slick bitch like Pamela," she stated flatly.

Nick nearly dropped the receiver. Was this the refined Elizabeth Mason? "Don't hold back, Lizzie," he said, laughing at her blunt language.

"Besides, I don't see what harm her experiment will do."

"What if her faculty friends find out she's experimenting on them without their knowledge or consent? Using them. I wonder if she's thought about that possibility. Your inestimable Dr. Harkness may find her experiment backfiring on her." He found the idea appealing.

"You wouldn't do anything rash, would you?" she asked, apprehensive at his change of tone. "You won't do anything to jeopardize her career?"

"Far be it from me to jeopardize her career." He laughed a short, humorless laugh. "I won't do anything unwarranted."

Elizabeth was so pleased with his tacit consent to take the job that the rather ambiguous nature of his promise did not register. "Then you'll do it? Can you make an audition Monday at four? I'm sure it will be just a formality, but it will give you a chance to meet Dr. Harkness."

"I'll be there."

"You're an angel," Elizabeth exclaimed gratefully.

"'Tis strange what a man may do,'" Nick quoted, "'And a woman may yet think him an angel.'"

"See! That's why I know you'll be perfect for the job. You can remember all that stuff and reel it off at the drop of a hat. Very impressive."

"He wrapped himself in quotations—as a beggar would enfold himself in the purple of Emperors." Now that he had taken up the challenge, he felt quite light-hearted.

"On the other hand," Elizabeth said, "you can get a little carried away at times. You know that, don't you?"

"'I hate quotations. Tell me what you know.'"

"I know that you are impossible. Stop it! I would love to listen to your nonsense all day, but I have appointments to keep."

"And miles to go before you sleep," he murmured wickedly.

"Nick!"

"Sorry, just practicing for the academic crowd."

"I expect you to be on your best behavior on Monday," she warned him.

"If I'm the rudest man you know, how good can that be?"

"Are you fishing for compliments? All right. When you are good, you are very, very good," she said, falling into the spirit of things.

"And when I am bad?"

"You are horrid!" she exclaimed triumphantly.

"Torrid, did you say?"

"Horrid!" With that, she slammed down the receiver and worked with a big smile on her face for the next half hour.

3

ELIZABETH KNEW the moment Nick arrived at the agency because suddenly all work ceased. The female agents who had been talking on the phone as he came in rolled their eyes in frustration, bored by calls that only a moment before had been interesting. The agents who were free soon circled Nick, each vying for his attention. Elizabeth strolled out of her office and stopped, shaking her head as she took him in. Normally he was impeccably dressed, a legacy of his clothing-store days, but today he was dressed in a pair of worn light brown cords that bagged at the knees and an equally ancient dark brown corduroy jacket with leather patches on the elbows. The collar of his white shirt was slightly frayed and gravy spots were visible on his brown plaid tie.

"Professor Taurage, I presume?"

"Got it in one."

"All that's missing is the pipe."

With a grin, Nick reached into his sagging jacket pocket and pulled out a huge bulldog pipe.

"Really, Nick," Elizabeth expostulated as they walked back to her office, "she's going to know you're mocking her."

"I'm just trying to make her feel at home," he protested with an injured air. Unable to maintain this fiction for long, he sat down and said, "She probably won't even notice."

Elizabeth was about to lecture him further when the receptionist buzzed her office to tell her that Dr. Harkness had arrived. She started to get up, but when she caught a glimpse of Susan, she sank back in her chair. "Oh, no!"

"What is it? Are you all right?" Elizabeth looked so stunned that Nick was afraid she had taken ill.

"I'm all right," she managed to say, "but look." She pointed toward the door.

He twisted around in his chair. He saw a young woman dressed in a light brown corduroy skirt, a dark brown corduroy blazer, and a white blouse with a plaid ribbon tied in a bow at her neck. "Professor Harkness, I presume?"

"Got it in one," she replied grimly.

Nick turned back to face her, his face lit up with repressed laughter. "Do you suppose she has a pipe in her purse?"

"Nicholas, this is no laughing matter. What are we going to do? She can't see you looking like that. How could you do it?"

"How was I to know she would show up wearing the regimental uniform? I thought it was a joke. Look, if I take off the jacket and tie, I'll be a bit informal but at least we won't look like the Bobbsey Twins: Their Collegiate Years."

"It will have to do, I suppose." Frowning at him, she went out to meet Susan while Nick shed his sartorial sarcasm.

Susan stood by the front door of the agency trying not to fidget or bolt. She had noticed a flurry of movement in Elizabeth Mason's office when she was announced and nervously wondered if anything was wrong. She wouldn't be here at all if she hadn't announced to Rich-

ard this morning that she hoped he wouldn't be too disappointed, but she had a date for the Faculty Club dinner
dance this year and couldn't go with him. His surprised
reaction, which she had accurately predicted, had simultaneously hurt, annoyed and pleased her. And now,
as they say in theatrical circles, she thought, the die is
cast. Or is it gambling circles? She mentally shrugged her
shoulders. Either would be appropriate for this madcap
scheme.

She had come here directly from a hectic day of teaching, student appointments and committee meetings, tired
and unprepared except for a brief pep talk from Molly.
She didn't even know what went on in an audition. Was
she supposed to question him about his previous experience? Was she supposed to pretend they were at the
party and improvise a conversation?

"Dr. Harkness," Elizabeth said, recalling her from her
agitated thoughts. "I'm glad you could make it. Would
you care for a cup of coffee before we get started?" When
Susan nodded, she poured strong black coffee into a
white mug that had the thespian masks on its sides and
handed it to her.

As a modern, educated woman, Susan naturally did
not believe in omens or superstitions; nevertheless, when
she found herself drinking from the crying face side of the
mug, she surreptitiously switched the mug from one
hand to the other so that the smiling face was turned toward her.

"Nick is already here," Elizabeth said as she let Susan
back to her office.

He stood up when the two women entered the room
and Susan thought, *he's so big.* While she had wanted
him to dwarf Richard, she had forgotten that he would
also overshadow her. It was not just his height that made

her feel like Alice in Wonderland after she had swallowed the entire contents of the little bottle labeled Drink Me. His wide shoulders, the muscular arms that she could detect even through his shirtsleeves, and the strength of his handshake were part of the heady brew.

"Dr. Harkness," he murmured in acknowledgement of Elizabeth's introduction. His lips were quirked into a beguiling smile.

Susan abruptly pulled her hand back. She could sense that he was a dangerous man. He would laugh at the strictures of the conventional world and his laughter would be infectious. Another time she might have been tempted to join in, but not now, not at this critical juncture in her career. She had too much to lose. She followed Elizabeth Mason to the audition room, keeping a safe distance from him.

After they were seated at a small square table in the centre of the room, Susan took a folded copy of Nick's résumé out of her briefcase. She smoothed it flat and pretended to study what she had already memorized. "You don't have a lot of experience," she observed, taking the initiative.

"Well, now, I guess that depends on what kind of experience you have in mind." His voice was husky with a hint of amusement hidden in its deep tones.

He hadn't expected to enjoy himself, but the minute he had seen her dressed in her cords and clutching her briefcase like a security blanket, he had relaxed his guard. He was prepared to have fun.

"I mean acting experience, of course," she replied sharply, wishing she were twenty years older and wore bifocals so she could peer over the rims and give him a properly quelling look.

"Of course."

"I see you were in a film for Northern State Power Company. What was that about and what part did you play?"

"It was an animated film about energy conservation and safety geared toward elementary schoolchildren." Nick pushed away from the table to give himself more leg room and tilted back in the chair until it balanced on two legs. "I did the voice-over for Rudy Kilowatt, the character who narrated the film."

"Rudy Kilowatt?" she asked, eyeing the precarious angle of his chair. As if to compensate, she sat straighter in her own chair, her feet planted firmly on the floor.

"He is the character who is the symbol of electricity. His head is a light bulb, his body an electric cord, and his legs are the prongs of a plug-in."

I can't bring Rudy Kilowatt to the Faculty Club, she silently groaned. Get out of this, now. "And how would that role qualify you to talk intelligently with college faculty?" she asked with raised eyebrows. As soon as the words were out she knew that she was in trouble. Nick's chair crashed down on all four legs as he leaned forward as if to see if she was in earnest. She took a deep breath and, summoning all the professional chutzpa she could manage, met his eyes unflinchingly.

"It will probably come in real handy when they want to talk about current events," he said mockingly.

Susan bit her cheek to keep from laughing. All right, so he was quick-witted as well as handsome, but could she trust him? Or would his irreverence get them both into trouble? One misspoken word or snipe from him at the Faculty Club would damn her as well as him, with far more devastating consequences. "You find life very amusing, don't you?" she said in a cool voice.

"Yes, I do. Don't you?"

"No, I don't." She felt a wave of sadness wash over her. Life hadn't been very amusing lately.

"Maybe I could remedy that," Nick found himself saying. It certainly wasn't what he had intended to say, but the stricken look that had flashed across her face had touched him. He felt an impulse to take her hands and whirl her around the room until she was flushed and disheveled.

"What do you mean?" The invitation implicit in the caress of his voice was unmistakable, but this was a business interview. She couldn't understand why he was flirting with her. Maybe that was the only way he knew how to deal with women. Or he was bored and flirting to pass the time. Or perhaps he felt sorry for her. None of these alternatives lightened Susan's mood.

Nick looked into her wary hazel eyes and threw caution to the wind. "I mean," he said, warming to his idea, "we could forget science and Humboldt College. We could go for a drive along the St. Croix Valley and enjoy the autumn leaves. 'A Book of Verses beneath the Bough, A Jug of Wine, A Loaf of Bread—and Thou.'"

"Are you seducing me, Mr. Taurage?" she asked incredulously.

"Apparently not," he sighed and wondered what on earth had possessed him to play the romantic fool with a woman who must have graduated Phi Beta Kappa from the Lizzie Borden Charm School.

This is all just a game for him, Susan thought, on the verge of angry tears. It isn't his life's work on the line. "Why are you doing this? Did you think it would be amusing?" She nearly spit the word out. "Well, I am not amused."

"I can see that."

The horrifying prospect of breaking down in front of him made her fire back, "Do you have so little confidence in your acting ability that you have to seduce every woman who interviews you for a job?"

"As a matter of fact, I have never had to audition for a woman before."

"That's quite obvious," she returned, realizing a beat too late that he was referring to more than job interviews.

"Why, thank you, Dr. Harkness. I'm glad my charms are so apparent."

"I think that about does it." She snapped her briefcase closed with a decisive click and started to stand up. "This audition is over. I shall lodge a complaint with Ms. Mason about your unprofessional conduct."

Nick caught her hand as she started to leave. "You've misunderstood," he said quickly, thinking Lizzie will skin me alive if I don't smooth things over. "I was to accompany you to a faculty dinner dance, was I not? To be your date? I thought the most convincing way to persuade you that I could do the job would be to slip into the role."

Susan sat back down and stared at him. "Oh. So you were acting?"

"Yes."

Susan discovered that, if she had been insulted before when he was trying to seduce her, she was even more insulted now that he was not.

"Do I get the job?" he asked with an engaging grin.

"Not so fast, Mr. Taurage. I knew you were acting." She glared at him, daring him to contradict her. Two could play this game.

"No!" he exclaimed in what he hoped was an appropriately chastened tone. His interest in her revived. So she was going to fight it out, was she?

"You're not the only one with acting ability," she announced loftily. "I, too, was just playing a part." Before she had time to panic about how she was going to carry this charade off, she had a flash of insight that struck with almost mystical force. The one jarring note in Nick's appearance became obvious to her. "As soon as I saw your choice of costume—you are in costume, aren't you?—I knew what you expected of me."

Nick wanted to applaud. She was quick.

"Your conception of academia, like your seduction technique," she continued scathingly, "is badly dated. The latter, in particular, is something one might expect from an aging Lothario who memorized Omar Khayyám as an undergraduate and had such great success with it then that he's been trying it ever since. Rather pathetic. I'm afraid if that's your style, my colleagues will make mincemeat out of you."

"Instead of mincemeat, would you settle for humble pie?" he asked, unexpectedly contrite. "I'm sorry if I've offended you."

What sort of trick was this, she wondered suspiciously. Was this another game?

"Shall we start over?" He extended his hand.

Short of refusing to accept his apology, which would be a churlish thing to do, she didn't see that she had any choice. She held out her hand and felt her wrath melt away in the warmth of his grasp. She was willing to ease hostilities but the problem was, robbed of her indignation, she didn't know how to proceed. She couldn't retreat into crisp professionalism again; he had effectively destroyed that option. She was stripped down and if he chose to mock her now, he would hurt her far beyond the power of any stranger to wound another. But if he chose to be kind . . .

Susan had a vision of herself sitting on a red-and-white-checked tablecloth on the grass, a jug of wine and a loaf of bread spread out in front of her.

"I think we'll skip the rest of your acting experience," she said, forcing herself back to reality. "It doesn't really matter anyway because you can just be yourself at the party." In the interests of their new fragile harmony, she refused to think about what would happen if Nick directed his sardonic wit against Fred Harrison's stuffiness.

"I promise to behave," Nick said as if he had read her mind.

"Your years in Europe, your connection with Roughwood Press, and house restoration work will give you plenty to talk about."

"How did you know about all that?"

"About what?"

"Europe, Roughwood, and my restoration projects—none of that is on my résumé."

"Elizabeth Mason told me."

"Ms. Mason is certainly a fount of information, isn't she?"

Susan was puzzled by the sudden tension in his voice. "Wasn't I supposed to know?" she asked.

"No, that's fine," he replied a bit absently. Had Elizabeth also told her about the Pamela fiasco? Surely not. "What else did she say about me?"

A smile crept to Susan's lips. "Well, she did say you were a modern-day Renaissance man."

"Good Lord!"

She laughed at the grimace on his face. "Surely you've been called worse things."

"Yes, I suppose I have. An aging Lothario was the most recent, I believe."

"I apologize for that."

"Please don't, for then I shall have to apologize for Elizabeth's gross exaggeration and we shall be caught in an endless echo of apologies."

"Then it's all settled. You'll do it?"

"Yes, but we're not done yet. Where did we meet? How long have we known each other? What do we usually do when we go out together? I need some background."

"I haven't thought any of that through," she said slowly. The realization that she was actually going to go through with this scheme was only just sinking in. "Is it really necessary?" She was reluctant to pile lies upon lies.

"People may ask and they'll wonder if I say we met while we were watching the dairy princesses being sculpted in butter at the State Fair and you say we met at the Minneapolis Public Library."

"I see what you mean." If she was going to do it, she might as well do it right. "All right, we met at the Minneapolis Public Library."

"So dull," he murmured sadly, shaking his head.

"Dull, but plausible," she pointed out, but the word dull had stung. "I was checking out *Civilization and its Discontents* by Sigmund Freud and you were checking out a movie, *Abbott and Costello Meet the Mummy*," she elaborated by way of revenge.

"I object!"

"You object to Abbott and Costello?"

"I object to *Abbott and Costello Meet the Mummy*. It's one of their lesser efforts."

"And what would you prefer?"

"*Abbott and Costello Meet Frankenstein*—the mad scientist. More appropriate, don't you think?"

She studied him clinically for a moment before saying, "I remember, the mad scientist who creates a monster. Hmmmm, perhaps you're right. It is more appropriate." She hurried on before he could deliver a rejoinder. "We started talking and ended up going out for a cup of coffee. That was about two weeks ago."

"You're so unromantic. Two weeks, three days, and twenty-two hours ago." Nick took up the story. "Since then we've gone out to dinner twice—the Black Forest Inn and the Rosewood Room, gone for a drive along the St. Croix Valley to see the leaves, and walked around Lake of the Isles in the rain. All right?"

"Yes," she said, busying herself, folding up his résumé and putting it back into her briefcase so she didn't have to look at him just then. "The dinner dance is this coming Saturday night at six-thirty. I live close to campus so you can come to my house and we can walk to school."

"What shall I wear?"

"Anything but brown cords."

"To err is human, to forgive divine," he reminded her.

"A suit and tie will do," she said relenting. "Now I must go and complete the business arrangements with Ms. Mason." She was halfway out the door when she heard Nick call her back.

"Susan."

She turned around, half afraid that he had changed his mind.

"I'm looking forward to Saturday night," he said simply.

She managed to nod and left the room muttering, the cure is worse than the disease.

4

IT RAINED ALL DAY Saturday, a relentless gray downpour that cast such a gloom over the city that the streetlights flickered off and on, uncertain whether it was night or day. Few people walked by Susan's house. Those who did brave the elements, dragged along by dogs straining at their leashes, hid behind big black umbrellas they carried in front of them like shields against the wind. She kept an anxious eye on the weather all day, but around five o'clock the sky began to clear and by six o'clock when she went upstairs to get ready for the Faculty Club dinner dance, the rosy sun in the west warmed the air with its departing light.

She put on her favorite dress, a simple lightweight wool with a gently tailored bodice and a belted full skirt that floated out around her like a bell when she ran down the stairs.

Everyone at Humboldt had seen it a dozen times over, but its rich green color and soft feminine lines suited her. A pair of delicately carved jade earrings completed her outfit. She cursorily examined herself in the mirror. Anticipation of the evening made her eyes sparkle and her cheeks were flushed with natural color. Not exactly luminous, but not bad, either.

High heels in hand, she went downstairs in her stocking feet and looked at the kitchen clock. Still a bit early. Maybe hiring a man for the night wasn't such a good idea, she worried belatedly as she paced the floor. Particularly when that man was Nicholas Taurage. Maybe sitting on the sidelines chatting to the senior faculty about pension plans wouldn't have been so bad. Now that she thought about it, she could work up a lot of enthusiasm about pension plans. Maybe... When the knock she had been waiting for finally sounded as loud as a judge's gavel on judgment day, she jumped so violently that she scared herself.

She opened the door. Nick was studying the seven coffee cans and buckets collecting the rain that was still dripping through the porch roof. By now she was so used to all the problems with her old house that she had forgotten how shabby it might look to an outsider. "'An ill-favored thing, sir, but mine own,'" she said a trifle defiantly.

He was dressed in an expensive-looking dark gray pin-striped suit with a tightly furled red rose pinned to the lapel. The brilliant blue-white of his silk shirt deepened his tan and intensified his dark eyes. Her qualms increased. This was no starving actor, grateful for work.

Before he could speak, a big drop fell from the ceiling onto his forehead. "You've missed one," he said, laughing as he pulled out a white linen handkerchief to wipe away the raindrop.

"Come on in." She stepped back, holding the door open with an extended arm. The entryway was narrow and she caught a hint of a clean masculine fragrance, as elusive and tantalizing as the scent of an herb in her garden, as he walked past her.

Nick was taken aback by Susan's house. Both the living room and the connecting dining room were completely bare save for a wall-to-wall carpet in the ugliest mustard color he had ever seen, and a built-in buffet which was probably made of oak but was presently disguised with mint-green paint. The brick fireplace was blackened with soot. "Have you just moved in?" he asked, his voice echoing in the emptiness.

"No. I've lived here about a year." He looked so prosperous that she didn't feel like confessing that she had spent every penny of her meager savings on the down payment and that her salary barely covered the mortgage payments. She couldn't afford furniture. In fact, she couldn't afford him! Susan had been shocked when Elizabeth Mason had told her the standard fee for a personal appearance, but she had been determined—even if it meant squeezing an already strangling budget.

"Then you must favor minimalist design," he observed with a smile before dropping the subject to Susan's relief. "This is for you." He handed her a small green florist box.

She opened the box and, nestled in the tissue paper, was a small cluster of red roses, companions to his own. "Thank you." She made an effort to be gracious and sophisticated, but she hadn't felt so awkward since junior high school.

"May I?" Nick asked, lifting the roses out of the box. Without waiting for an answer, he expertly tucked them into the brown curls framing her face and stood back to inspect the results. "Very nice."

Her temple tingled where his fingertips had brushed against her. "Thank you, Nick. They're lovely, but it wasn't necessary to bring me flowers. I mean, it's not as if this is a real date or anything like that. This is work for both of us." So much for being gracious.

"I'll try not to have a good time," he promised tartly.

"Please have Elizabeth Mason add the cost of the roses to my bill," she blundered on.

"Fine."

"Shall we go then? Just let me get a notepad to stick into my purse. I might want to jot down some notes during the course of the evening."

"Tell me more about your experiment," Nick said as they walked toward the campus.

"Oh, I don't want to bore you."

"You won't."

Did he suspect anything? she wondered uneasily. She knew her so-called experiment was feeble sociology, but did he? How could he? She decided to cover up her tracks with a layer of verbiage and jargon so thick, he couldn't see through it. "I'm using a method called participant observation in which researchers participate in the situation they are studying. The advantage is that since the researchers are part of the group, they are privy to the group's secrets. They have an insider's view, which allows them to see and hear things they wouldn't under more formal, structured conditions. The disadvantage is that it is harder to remain objective." She felt safe talking about methodology. She taught the course and could lecture to him for an entire semester if he cared to listen.

"What do you hope to prove in this particular experiment?"

She began to walk faster. The sooner they got to the dance, the better. "I'm afraid I can't tell you," she answered. "Social scientists have learned that their expectations can alter the results of an experiment. Subjects say what they think the researchers want to hear. It's best that you don't know the purpose of my experiment to preserve the integrity of the interaction." There, if he swallowed that, she was home free.

Nick lapsed into silence. Her explanation sounded plausible enough, but he couldn't shake the feeling that she had left something unstated—something very important. A horrible thought struck him. Was history going to repeat itself? He stopped in the middle of the sidewalk, frozen by his suspicions. "Am I the subject of your experiment?" he demanded, tightly gripping her arm. "Am I?"

"No, of course not." She twisted away from him, startled by his sudden hostility. "I've told you. I'm observing my colleagues." When he still looked disbelieving, she asked, "What makes you think you're the subject of my research?"

"You won't say much about this experiment of yours. It makes me wonder what you have to hide." His expression was harsh and unforgiving.

What would he say if he found out that she had been desperate enough to hire a date? Her face burned with humiliation. "I think the shoe is on the other foot," she shot back. "What are *you* trying to hide? What are you afraid I'll find out about you?"

"Look, I just signed on to attend this function with you. I didn't sign on to be psychoanalyzed by some textbook toreador."

"Maybe this isn't such a good idea. Do you want to just call it off?" She didn't know which answer she wanted to hear more. "I'll be happy to pay you for your time in either case."

"What about your experiment?"

"What do you care?" she asked pointedly. "How about it? Shall we call it quits? It's entirely up to you."

Elizabeth's jibe ran through his mind. "Pamela Whitbread certainly did a job on you, didn't she?" Could he trust Susan? Standing there at the edge of campus, scowling at Susan, he finally had to admit that Lizzie might be right. He had gone out with many women since Pamela, but he had never allowed these affairs to progress beyond a certain point. He made love with a light touch, tantalizing but ultimately elusive.

Once he had agreed to go to the Faculty party with Susan, he had envisioned matching wits with her in a delightful game of pretend in which no one won or lost. He intended to keep it light as he had always done, but already his control was slipping. His old fear had returned. Too late, he realized that the game was real and he could lose.

He looked at Susan twisting a strand of hair around her finger as she waited for his decision. In the short hours that he had known her, she had intrigued him more than any other woman he had met in the last five years. He wanted to believe that she was different from Pamela. "I'll do it," he said and took her hand to seal the bargain. Still holding her hand, he resumed walking.

"You're sure?" Susan asked, dragging her feet. She would rather face Richard and FTP alone than endure Nick's suspicions the whole evening.

"Yes, I'm sure." He said it with such quiet determination that she relaxed.

Susan felt like an undergraduate again as they strolled along the dusky tree-lined sidewalk. There was no place she would rather be than a college campus in the fall. Fresh air, fresh faces, everyone full of energy, ready to learn. By spring, the excitement would have worn off. Faculty and students alike would be tired and cranky and even the most inspiring text failed to inspire when nearly nude sunbathers were stretched out on blankets just outside the classroom window. But for now, the campus was alive with purpose.

Susan's sense of humor reasserted itself as they walked through the campus hand in hand like a couple of love-sick teenagers too young for sex and too old for punching each other on the arm. In retrospect, the confrontation she and Nick had took on comical proportions and she laughed out loud as she recalled his accusation.

"What is it?" he asked as they climbed the Faculty Club steps.

"Textbook toreador?" she said with raised eyebrows.

"It was the best I could come up with in the heat of the moment." He grinned and began to sing from *Carmen* under his breath, "Toreador, en garde, toreador."

Susan joined in on the chorus and with a flourish, they marched into the Faculty Club, through the large flagstone foyer, and down the three steps into the Great Hall. Many faculty and their spouses were already standing at the bar or sitting in scattered groups, having cocktails before dinner. President Turner and his wife stood at the foot of the stairs, greeting people as they arrived.

Susan nudged Nick into silence, but before she had a chance to introduce him, Melissa Turner, an effusive woman some twenty years younger than her husband, held out her hands and pulled him forward, kissing him on the cheek. "Nick! I didn't expect to see you here. What a surprise! Ray, this is Nicholas Taurage. He's one of the volunteers at The Literacy Center."

The president shook hands with Nick. "I'm glad to meet you. Melissa has often mentioned you."

"I only put in a few hours a week. It's your wife who is the energy and spirit behind the operation."

"There!" Melissa turned to her husband. "Didn't I tell you he was a perceptive young man?"

Ray Turner smiled indulgently at her. She was easily the same age or even a few years younger than Nick.

"I only hope, sir, that she doesn't manage you as ruthlessly as she does us," Nick said.

"You're right, Melissa. He is perceptive," the president commented with a dry laugh.

Melissa wrinkled her nose at the two men and turned to Susan. "I didn't know you knew Nick."

"I haven't known him for long. We just met a few weeks ago."

"At the State Fair," Nick contributed.

"Well, we don't want to hold up the line," Susan said brightly, taking his arm and moving away. "What happened to the Minneapolis Public Library?" she demanded on their way to the bar. "And why didn't you tell me you were on such friendly terms with the president's wife?"

"I didn't know I was. I'm not sure I ever knew her last name. And I would have never pictured her as a college president's wife. At the center, we call her Charo."

They had no sooner gotten their drinks than Molly rushed up. "Hi!" she said to Susan although her eyes were fixed on Nick.

"Nick, this is Molly Higgins. She's in the English department. Molly, this is Nick Taurage."

"Come sit with us," Molly said as she shook his hand.

Nick followed Susan and Molly as they made their way through the growing crowd of people. "I've staked us out a place right by the door so people can see us when they come in the room and I've managed to corral both Phillip Hunter and Ken Bjorklund," Molly whispered to Susan. "That's two members of FTP taken care of. I've arranged for you to sit down to dinner with two others—Louis Hess and Steve Birnbaum. You're on your own with the other two."

"You are incredible," Susan whispered back.

"By the way, you're not the only one on the political prowl tonight. Watch out for Will Lambert."

Susan glanced around the room and saw Will dogging the steps of Herman Blandish, the chairman of the sociology department. Will was on a temporary contract at Humboldt, replacing one of Susan's colleagues who was on sabbatical. That meant next year he would be out of a job again. She would be glad to see him go. With his long, thin face, white-blond hair and pale blue eyes, he reminded her of an albino weasel and he was probably about as trustworthy as well. He was pleasant enough to her on the surface but she knew that underneath he was hoping she would be denied tenure so he could step into her position.

Taking note of his presence, Susan turned back to Molly. "Is Richard here yet?"

"Not yet." They reached the group. "I think there's room here on the couch with Miguel and me if we squeeze a bit."

Squeeze didn't quite capture it. If Nick so much as tapped a toe, Susan would have felt his muscles flex, for his thigh was pressed bone for bone, sinew for sinew, against hers. She felt as though all the sensation in her body was centered on the body heat that emanated between them. She stirred uneasily; she hadn't counted on this reaction.

"All right?" Nick rested his arm on the back of the couch behind her in order to give them a fraction more space. "It was kind of your friend to save us a seat," he said with a shadow of a smile. There were dozens of empty chairs scattered all over the room.

"Yes, wasn't it?" Well, subtlety had never been Molly's strong suit. She willed her head to conquer her body's betrayal and succeeded sufficiently enough to turn to the business at hand. "Let me introduce you to the others," she said smoothly. During the course of the introductions, it turned out that Nick and Phillip shared an interest in Japanese Kabuki theater and Susan discovered that Ken and Shirley Bjorklund were from the same part of Wisconsin as she was. Soon they were exchanging childhood reminiscences, while Nick and Phillip compared notes on various performances they had seen. Molly, Miguel, and Teresa Hunter kept happily occupied discussing the new laws regulating child care facilities until they were interrupted by a loud gong announcing dinner. Glancing at her watch, Susan was surprised to see that they had been talking for nearly forty-five minutes.

"Don't you just love it?" Molly remarked when she heard the gong. "It's so colonial, like something out of *The King and I*. Shall we go up?" The dining room was on the second floor and everyone was moving toward the front stairs when Richard and Michelle appeared, framed by the doorway. All eyes turned in their direction. "It's an art, isn't it?" Molly muttered to Susan.

Richard looked good, Susan automatically noted. He must have bought a new suit for the occasion and his hair looked carefully coiffed, but he was clearly the supporting actor of the pair. Michelle was wearing a thigh-length red dress made of some sleek material that caressed every curve of her body. Susan would have broken an ankle in ten paces if she had to wear the four-inch backless spike heels that graced Michelle's feet and she could have sworn that she could count every individual long and delicate eyelash fanning Michelle's high cheekbones when she blinked her big blue eyes. "She is breathtaking," Susan said in a low tone to Molly. "You have to give her credit for that."

"I rather think Richard means to take the credit for that. He won't be too pleased when he finds out I've put him at a table in a dark corner of the dining room with the biggest bores on campus." She looked smug. "Let's go eat. All this plotting has given me an appetite."

Dinner was not as smooth sailing as the social hour had been. Susan sat next to Louis Hess, an eccentric bachelor who was chair of the computer science department and who had few other interests. She listened to his monotonous recitation of the latest hardware and software available on the market with a polite smile pasted on her lips, filling in the infrequent silences with encouraging noises.

She avoided looking at Nick who had laughed when Hess asked her if she was familiar with Lotus and she replied, only half paying attention, "Yes, it's a yoga position, isn't it?" Luckily, after a moment's stunned silence, he joined in Nick's laughter and now believed Susan to be the wittiest woman he had ever met.

Nick didn't have much easier going. He discovered that Steve Birnbaum's wife, Karen, hated faculty parties and resented her husband for insisting she attend. She always came out of some remnant sense of wifely duty, but her physical presence was her only concession. She wouldn't talk, she wouldn't drink, she wouldn't dance. Steve made things worse by speaking for her. "Oh, good, Karen likes wild rice," he announced when they were served dinner. When Nick asked her about herself, Steve answered, "Karen is a housewife," and that ended that. Nick learned that her favorite book was *Gone With The Wind*, that she was originally from Colorado, and that she had always wanted to travel to England—all without her uttering a single word.

Toward the end of the meal, while they were still drinking their coffee before the dance began, Susan excused herself to go to the ladies' room. Nick, sorely tried by the strained conversation, turned to Steve. "Does Karen need to go, too?"

The set lines in Karen's face twitched, stilled, then twitched again as she took in the shock on Steve's face. "I don't need to go, thank you." This was the first complete sentence she had spoken at a faculty gathering in fifteen years. "Steven, would you please get me a Scotch and soda?" she asked her husband who immediately jumped up and hurried toward the bar. "We may always end up doing things his way," she said to Nick after he was gone, "but I make damn sure he doesn't enjoy it."

"I would have thought you could do better than that," Nick replied with a shrug.

"Perhaps I can. The question is whether I will or not." She lapsed into silence.

Another crisis averted, Susan walked shakily toward the ladies' room. Molly followed her in. "How are we doing?" Susan asked her. Molly had arranged to sit directly behind them and had spent more time listening to the conversation at their table than her own.

"Piece of cake!" Molly exclaimed, eyes shining with delight.

"I'm glad you're having so much fun."

"Susan, it really is going amazingly well. Nick is wonderful. You were lucky to find him—he's perfect. Now all you have to do is face Richard and talk to Fred Harrison and Roger Perkins. I only wish I could tell somebody about this. We're really going to pull it off!"

The party moved downstairs again for the dance. While the guests dined, the chairs and couches scattered throughout the Great Hall had been lined against the walls or rearranged in rather crowded conversational groupings. The Humboldt Swing Band had set up in a corner opposite the bar, and were playing their first number. As usual, everyone was waiting for everyone else to start dancing.

"Shall we break the ice?" Susan asked Nick. Ordinarily she, too, would have hung back but here was another chance to be visible. She waved at Fred Harrison as they walked out onto the dance floor.

"I hope I didn't mess things up for you back there," Nick asked, looking down at her. He was a good dancer, moving with such easy confidence that Susan soon relaxed in his arms and matched his grace with her own.

"I think we share the honors on that score," she answered, then stiffened as she saw Richard swing Michelle out onto the floor and steer her in their direction.

Nick followed her gaze but saw nothing more remarkable than an ordinary-looking bespectacled man dancing with a woman who looked like a model. What was it about them that made Susan stumble? Was the man a campus bigwig? A lover? This time, it was he who missed a step.

When the music stopped, Richard and Michelle were standing next to them. Susan forced a cheerful smile on her face. "Hello, Richard."

"Susan, I've been looking for you. Why don't we four sit out the next dance and get acquainted?"

Once they were seated and introduced, Richard announced proudly, "Michelle is going to model the new spring collection."

"Nick is co-owner of Roughwood Press," Susan countered. "The *New York Times* just selected them as one of the ten best regional publishers in the country."

"Michelle studied dance with Nancy Hauser," Richard returned.

"Oh, did I mention that Nick was a consultant for the restoration of the James J. Hill House?"

Richard had opened his mouth to reply when Nick abruptly stood up. "What is this, dueling résumés?" he demanded. "Michelle, would you care to dance while these two say whatever they have to say to each other?"

Richard and Susan watched Nick and Michelle walk away and begin dancing. They made a beautiful couple.

"Now you've done it," Richard accused.

"You started it!" She flung back.

"I did not!"

"Yes, you did!" It only took a second for both of them to hear what they were saying.

"Oh, Susan!" Richard clutched his sides, aching with laughter.

"I think I had this same conversation with my older brother a trillion billion times!" she gasped.

When they had stopped giggling, Richard said, "Susan, I don't want to start anything, but where did you get this guy?"

"What do you mean?" She hunched her shoulders against the renewed tension.

"I mean, do you know anyone who knows him? How do you know he is who he says he is? Did you call Roughwood to check him out?"

"I can't believe this."

"There are a lot of con men running around victimizing innocent women and I don't want you to be one of them."

"Melissa Turner can vouch for him, all right? Is that good enough for you? Why does there have to be a catch?"

"All right, all right." He held up his hands in surrender. "What do you say we go cut in on our partners?" As they reached the edge of the dance floor, he caught her arm. "Susan, I said that about Nick—" he shifted his feet nervously and then, with an effort, met her eyes, "—because I care about you."

"I know you do, Richard," she said. But I had wanted you to want me as well, she recalled sadly as she bid a final farewell to that misguided daydream.

"Then all is forgiven?" he joked awkwardly. "We're still friends?"

Instinctively she knew that he was not referring to the conversation that had just taken place. This was as close as he could come to an apology for his silence when she had told him she loved him. Relief conquered sadness. Friend didn't sound like such a bad word anymore. "All is forgiven." She hugged him and didn't care how many members of FTP saw.

Was it possible that she was going to break out of this long spell of hard times? For the first time in nearly three years, things were falling into place as they should. Her face was glowing with the hope of happiness as she walked out onto the dance floor, humming along with the music.

Nick wordlessly relinquished Michelle in exchange for Susan when she cut in. The touching little reconciliation scene between Richard and her had not escaped his notice. When she slipped into his arms, he looked away from her as one might avoid staring directly into the naked sun and as soon as the music ended, he stepped back a pace.

"I'm afraid Richard and I behaved rather badly," Susan ventured with a wry glance at Nick's cross face. Impulsively she reached up to stroke away the tension etching his jawline. Her fingertips tingled from the feel of his warm, smooth skin.

An unexpected possessiveness burned through him at her touch. He captured her wrist and held it immobile.

He tried to control his urge to kiss her until he had erased the memory of Richard from her body and mind. Frustrated by public proprieties, he swore under his breath and limited himself to lightly brushing her open palm with his mouth.

His simple gesture left Susan weak-kneed and strangely shaken. She was only dimly aware that the band had begun to play again. When Nick pulled her into his arms, she gave herself up to his embrace, the fragrance of the rose in his lapel, and the waltz. She had worked hard enough for one night. Academic politics receded from her consciousness as she closed her eyes and concentrated on the sensual movement of his body against hers.

"Susan, look," Nick whispered.

Reluctantly, she opened her eyes and followed his gaze. Ten feet away, Steve and Karen Birnbaum were dancing together. He held his wife tentatively as if he couldn't quite believe his good fortune. Susan could see from the astonished faces of the other people dancing that no one else quite believed it, either. Karen smiled enigmatically at Nick.

"Well, well," Susan marveled. "What wonders have you wrought, Mr. Taurage?" She glanced up at him and then quickly down again, catching her breath, for she had seen the promise of other wonders in his eyes.

The band did a neat segue into a fox-trot. Without any hesitation, Nick adjusted to the change in tempo and they continued dancing. Neither of them spoke, unwilling to break the spell that seemed to remove them from the world around them, a world of politics, gossip, and rivalry. They were quite alone, dancing through the night in each other's arms.

"May I cut in?"

Now who was this? Nick wondered irritably. Susan knew entirely too many people. He studied the interloper, a short portly man dressed in a shiny brown suit. He was no threat, Nick decided and stepped aside.

Susan sighed inwardly as she was duly passed from Nick to Fred Harrison, her mentor and nemesis. Over Fred's shoulder, she could see eagle-eyed Molly intercept Nick and lead him over to Roger Perkins, another member of the English department and the only remaining FTP representative to be lobbied. She had fooled herself into believing she was on a *real* date. But there was no escape from politics.

"I'm glad to see you took my advice," Fred said as they swerved and dipped their way across the floor. "Keep up the good work."

He twirled her around and, for a moment, in the blur of faces, Susan picked out Will Lambert staring at them. She was startled by the unmasked hostility of his expression, but by the time she was facing his direction again, he had turned his back to her and she was unsure whether she had actually seen his antagonism or made it up. Nevertheless, he was an additional reminder that there was work to be done. No more impossible daydreams, no more fairy tales.

"What do you think of the Academic Policy Committee's recommendation that we abolish the pass/fail grading option for electives?" she asked Fred. He happily outlined his position on pass/fail grading options for the rest of the dance.

She joined Nick, Molly and Roger when the dance was through. Nick moved over on the leather settee so she could sit next to him. She sank with a sigh of relief and kicked off her shoes.

"How was your dance?" he asked with a sympathetic smile. He had been surreptitiously watching Susan and Fred the whole time. "Or perhaps I should rephrase the question. What was it?"

"Fred is kind of a free-form dancer." She fortified herself with a long swallow of the drink Nick had ordered for her. She was acutely aware that his hand was resting lightly on her knee. "Did Roger tell you that he is working on a book on Minnesota writers?" she asked in a businesslike tone of voice. "It sounds like just the sort of thing Roughwood Press would be interested in publishing."

Nick withdrew his hand. "Indeed?"

"I was going to contact the Press when I was farther along with it," Roger said.

"What authors are you studying?" Nick asked politely.

"That has been one of my main problems," Roger admitted. "F. Scott Fitzgerald wrote *Tender is the Night* in St. Paul, but is he a Minnesota writer? I don't think so."

"But does a writer have to write about Minnesota to be counted as a Minnesota writer?" Molly interjected. "That seems unnecessarily restrictive. Does he or she have to live here? What about someone like Rebecca Hill who divides her time between Georgia and Minnesota?"

Arguing over definitions was a favorite pastime in academia, a preoccupation that quickly bored Nick. He sat there, caught between the pair of English professors ruminating over Minnesota authors like two cows chewing their cuds. It was a standard, predictable conversation until Susan broke in. "What about Pamela Whitbread?"

Nick felt the color drain from his face.

"You are referring to her first novel, *Fumbling the Ball*, I suppose." Roger looked thoughtful. "That would be an interesting selection. It certainly attracted a lot of local and national attention at the time. What do you think, Nick?"

He shrugged, unable to speak. A bit of attention. Twenty-six weeks on the *New York Times'* bestseller list. Universally acclaimed by critics. "A modern-day *Main Street*." "Devastating." "Magnificently mean." "Bravo, Dr. Whitbread, bravo."

"It was all the rage when I was in graduate school," Susan continued. "We loved it."

Oh, Susan, Nick protested, *not you, too*. He felt a great pressure building up in his chest, crushing his hopes, forcing bitter remembrance through his veins. He wanted to make his escape but Susan wasn't finished.

She shifted forward to the edge of the settee as if she might jump up at any moment and pace the floor, propelled by the energy of her thoughts. "It was such a popular book then, but have any of you read it recently?"

No one had.

"Well, that says something already," she commented. "I reread it last summer and it is trite, badly dated, and venomous beyond belief. You could do a long overdue critique of it, Roger."

The stone weight pressure in Nick's chest lightened and floated away.

"I couldn't believe that my friends and I had ever thought it was the most wonderful novel ever written." Susan was serious, shaking her head at their gullibility, but then a mischievous smile broke through. "We were like sharks joining in a feeding frenzy."

"Susan," Nick burst out fervently, leaning toward her and grasping her hands, "will you marry me?"

5

IT WAS AS IF the four of them had been playing Red Light, Green Light and Nick had suddenly yelled Red Light. Molly had just bent over to put her glass down on the coffee table and remained petrified in that position, her fingers clutching the glass. Roger looked like the village idiot with his mouth gaping in astonishment and Susan's smile became the smile permanently fixed on a Barbie doll, forever young and bright.

Laughter bubbled through Nick like champagne and spilled out over the three of them, washing away their shock.

"D-d-didn't you like *Fumbling the Ball*, either?" Susan stammered. She was sure her heart was thudding audibly to the others. Aware that Molly and Roger were still staring at them, she unobtrusively pulled her hands away from Nick's grasp and slid over on the settee to put some distance between them.

"No, not much." He had never noticed before how beautiful she was. She didn't have Pamela Whitbread's classical elegance or her polished diamond hard edges; she was a black opal reflecting light in a play of colors.

"The band is packing up for the night," Molly interrupted nervously, as if she were worried that Nick was getting too carried away playing the devoted escort.

Roger stood up to go, hiding a yawn behind the back of his hand. "Nick, it was nice to meet you."

"You leave Pamela Whitbread out of it and we'd be happy to see a proposal for your book," Nick told him.

"We should be going, too," Susan said, looking around. The crowd had thinned out until only the die-hard dancers and talkers remained. All the FTP members except Roger had already gone home. Her work was finished for the evening.

"Let me just go say goodbye to Melissa." Nick stroked the back of her hand with his finger as he got up. His touch was hypnotic and Susan had to struggle to pay attention to Roger who had lingered for a second.

"Thank you for plugging my book, Susan," he said as soon as Nick was out of earshot. "I won't forget it." He shook her hand gratefully, then he, too, took his leave.

"What a night!" Molly exclaimed.

"A Cinderella at the ball night," Susan agreed happily.

"You sparkled."

"I shimmered."

"You achieved luminosity!"

"I was scintillating."

"You were brilliant."

"I was as visible as the North Star on a moonless night."

They grinned at each other, coconspirators in an academic game of intrigue.

"Nick was worth every penny," Molly added deliberately.

Susan's grin abruptly vanished.

Molly's worst fears were confirmed. "Time for a little reality therapy," she said in the grim voice used by those who are about to deliver hard truths to those who really don't want to hear them. "You told me that you read too many fairy tales when you were growing up and I believe it! Your night at the ball wasn't brought to you courtesy of a fairy godmother and her magic wand. You are paying for this evening with your hard-earned money, cold cash, remember? You hired Nick to play a part and he did it very well, too well, damn him. And now the party's over. It's strictly cinders and ashes from here on out, Susan. Don't forget that."

"How can I forget it when I have friends like you and Richard to remind me?" She was immediately contrite when she saw the hurt expression on Molly's face. "I'm sorry." She let out a deep sigh. "You're right. I can't afford to let my imagination run wild."

"Maybe he will call you for a real date after this is over," Molly suggested hopefully, completely reversing course. She couldn't stand to see all the sparkle extinguished in Susan's eyes.

"Maybe, maybe not." She kissed Molly on the cheek and joined Nick.

He noticed that she was subdued on the way home. "Tired?" he asked gently.

She didn't think she would be able to sleep a wink all night, but it was an easy refuge. "Yes." Tired of being alone, she wanted to add. Tired of focusing entirely on school. She knew that, despite the political tension and triumph of the evening, what she would most remember was the feel of Nick's arms around her as they danced together.

He tucked her arm through his as if to steady her weary steps and didn't intrude upon her silence with further conversation.

His touch was both comforting and alarming and she discovered that she didn't want it to stop. Maybe she didn't have to give up so easily. Maybe retreating was just cowardice masquerading as common sense. But did she have the nerve to say something, to return his touch with her own?

Nick walked by her side, absorbed in his own thoughts. This was new territory for him, with uncharted emotions. Reckless exhilaration warred with battle-won caution and left him at a standstill, biding his time. When they arrived at her house, he came into the porch with her, delaying his departure, while she dug in her purse for her keys.

"Good night, Nick. Thank you for your help," she said stiffly. She couldn't go through with it. She just didn't have the nerve to make a move. If she hadn't hired him, it would be different. But not under these circumstances. She didn't know if she was more angry with herself or with him for setting off these disturbing feelings in her. "I'll tell Ms. Mason that you did a very good job." Let him know that she knew he was just acting.

Her cool dismissal decided him. He caught her by the shoulders as she opened the door and turned her toward him and bent his head.

She automatically closed her eyes and waited for that first delicious brush of his lips on hers, but it never came. Slowly she opened her eyes again, tears gathering behind the lids. She had given herself away so quickly. The tears vanished when she saw the expression in his eyes as he stood there looking at her. No one had ever looked at her in quite that way before.

The tightly furled roses he had placed in her hair at the beginning of the evening had opened in the warmth of the Faculty Club. He reached up, plucked a loose petal, wrapped the petal around his forefinger and caressed her trembling lower lip with it. She could feel its delicate fibers, smell its rich perfume. He traced a rose-scented path along the contours of her cheekbones, her eyebrows, and the delicate skin at the corner of her eyes, all the time watching her, watching the pulse pound in her throat, which set off an echoing beat in him.

It was only then that he kissed her. The petal fluttered forgotten to the floor as he buried his hands in her hair and tilted her face. Her lips were as soft to the touch as the rose. He kissed her lightly at first, savoring the teasing touch, which left them both hungering for more. He pulled her closer, wanting her to feel the desire she aroused in him. But instead of coaxing him with her body to abandon his restraint as he wanted her to do, she struggled to free herself from his arms. He let her go, trying to stifle the loss he immediately felt.

Susan was breathing as heavily as if she had just been running. Breaking free had taken an act of will she didn't know she was capable of, but it was either that or be consumed by him. When he caressed her, the strength had melted out of her body, replaced by a molten center that now erupted in a heated accusation. To protect herself from what she wanted, she turned her anger on him. "Will this cost me extra?" she demanded. "Will it be itemized on my bill? What as, I wonder?"

"Hazard pay!" he snapped back out of frustration.

The tension was too much; something inside her snapped. Anger and passion forced a new metal in her impervious to rebuff. She felt daring, as bold as she had never been bold before, as out of character as this night was out of the ordinary.

"When I receive the bill, will it say, 'Account payable for services rendered'? Isn't that how it goes?" she asked coolly in a voice she barely recognized as her own. "Tell me, what services do you render, Mr. Taurage?" She stroked his shoulders, chest, and arms appraisingly, like prospective buyers at a horse auction might run their hands up and down a stallion's flank, needing to feel as well as see before they put their money down.

"Susan," Nick said in a husky voice, "why don't we stop playing games? We both know what we want. Let's go inside." He made a move to step around her into the house, but she stopped him with the flat of her palm pressed against his chest.

"She who pays the piper calls the tune," she rebuked him silkily. She grasped his tie and pulled his head down for another kiss, but this time she was in charge. She bit his lower lip and tasted his sweet mouth. She kissed him until she was content with kisses no longer. Then, still facing him and holding on to his tie, she backed into the house, pulling him after her.

"Susan," he expostulated.

"Shhh." She locked the door behind them and motioned him to follow her up the stairs. In her bedroom, she turned to him and loosened his tie. His arms automatically reached out to encircle her, but she pushed them away, shaking her head at him. Leisurely, deliberately, she undressed him; his tie, jacket and shirt fell into a pile on the floor beside the bed. When he was naked to the waist, she stopped. With the tip of her tongue, she licked the outline of his collarbone and kissed the vulnerable hollow above and below it. She ran her hands down his arms, feeling his hard, well-developed biceps quiver involuntarily at her touch.

When she slowly unbuckled his belt, he was unable to control a groan that escaped from deep within his throat. "Enough." He tore at the buttons on her dress to hasten her torturous progress.

"No!" She stepped back. If he were to touch her, she knew she would be lost. They would fling themselves on the bed and it would be over far too quickly. She wanted to savor the feel of his warm skin against her lips and fingers. She wanted to torment him with her touch until he wanted her as much as she wanted him.

"I'm leaving. No woman taunts me like this." Nick's voice was roughened with thwarted desire. He rebuckled his belt, picked up his discarded clothing and started to walk away.

Susan caught up with him at the doorway. She put her arms around his waist from behind to stop him from leaving. Her cheek pressed against his shoulder blade, she drew him close to her until he could feel the buttons of her dress branding his flesh. The soft pressure of her rounded breasts against his back robbed him of his rebellion and Susan felt him gradually relax against the curves of her body. Her hands roved over his chest and followed the matt of hair as it narrowed on its downward path. He did not resist this time as she unfastened his belt buckle and slid the remainder of his clothing down his thighs. Impatiently kicking away his pants, shoes and socks, Nick turned and faced her, his nakedness a striking contrast to her formal dress. Susan's sharp intake of breath when she saw him went a long way toward assuaging his male pride.

She retreated to the bed and he advanced, step by step, in a silent tango that set a primitive rhythm pounding through their veins. At the bed's edge, she stopped. "Undress me without touching me," she said, daring him to refuse.

Nick's eyes flashed, but he could not draw back now. He undressed her so slowly that she began to understand his earlier rebellion. Her skin had become extraordinarily sensitive; the merest grazing of his fingertips and the movement of silken garments and cool air against her exposed flesh made her shiver. When she finally stood before him, as naked as he, she said, "Now lie down on the bed."

"You'll go too far," he warned. He made no move toward the bed, just stood rooted to the spot, clenching and unclenching his fists.

Susan knew that a single wrong move from her would unleash his barely controlled sexual fury. "Lie down on the bed, Nick," she repeated in the cool, firm tone lion tamers use when they are confronted with a defiant beast.

Cornered by his need for her, he did. "You will pay for this," he threatened in a low voice.

"I already have," she reminded him. She was trembling with excitement as she looked at him reclining against the ruffled white sham pillows at the head of her bed. His arms were casually crossed behind his head, baring his expanse of chest, but his right leg was bent, as if he was trying to shield his erection from her. A small smile on her lips, Susan put her hand on his knee and gently pushed down until he was entirely exposed.

She sat down beside him, her hip pressed against his, just looking at him, at his sex, and suddenly she felt shy and inhibited. She had been merely playing an exciting game up till now but this, this was for real. What was going to happen next could have consequences far beyond this night. As much as she wanted him, she couldn't risk pregnancy or disease for the sake of a few hours of escape.

"I can't do it," she said abruptly, standing up and walking away.

Susan's retreating nakedness acted like a red flag to Nick's desire. Misinterpreting her change of heart, he charged after her and twirled her around. "I warned you that you would go too far," he gritted out. "You can't tease me like this and get away with it." He swept her up in his arms and carried her back to bed.

"No, Nick!"

The panic in her voice cut through his single-minded determination to possess her. "What's wrong?" he demanded, a little more impatiently than he intended. He breathed a deep sigh of frustration. "What's wrong?" he asked, more gently this time.

She groped for the words to tell him but everything seemed too clinical, too cold, calculated, and somehow medicinal. "I . . . I . . . I'm not prepared," she managed to say, avoiding his eyes.

"Don't worry, darling," he promised fiercely. "I'm going to make sure that you're good and prepared." With a quick movement, he laid down beside her and rolled over, carrying her with him until she found herself on her back pinned to the bed by a muscular leg lying across her thighs. He raised on his elbow. "Now," he said fiercely, reveling in her helplessness, "it's my turn to tease." Holding her immobile, he kissed her and caressed her, all the while demanding, "do you like this?" Her body arched upward, muscles straining toward his touch. "Yes, I can see that you do."

"Nick, please," she implored, half out of her mind with desire. Her green eyes, nearly black with heated emotion, were dilated with excitement. Nick could see a man reflected there, a man so savage that he barely recognized him. He looked beyond the man and for a brief, still moment, he believed that he could see deep within the woman, to the red-hot core, the pulsating heart, the tightly clenched muscles, the surge of warm blood.

"Are you prepared now?" It was a rhetorical question.

"That's not what I meant," she gasped out, simultaneously mortified and frantic with need. She closed her eyes in order to be able to say the words. "I meant safe sex. You know...a condom." A silence followed and Susan's eyes flew open to see if she had offended him.

Instead he was looking at her with something resembling tenderness. "I wouldn't do anything to hurt you," he said softly before getting up and crossing the room to where his pants lay in a heap on the floor. When he came back, he ripped open the foil package.

Susan trembled with anticipation. There would be no holding back now. She could let go.

He moved over her and entered her with a slow, strong stroke, slipping his arms under her, around her, so he could hold her as closely as possible. "I may be wearing a condom," he whispered teasingly in her ear, "but sex with me is never safe."

She wrapped her arms and legs around him until they were so intertwined that one's movement was indecipherable from the other's. "I knew from the start that you were a dangerous man."

They lay quite still, looking at each other, but the overwhelming relief they felt at finally coming together after the torment they had inflicted upon each other was quickly replaced by a new urgency.

Susan could hear herself crying out inarticulate sighs, sexual words, commands, and pleading as Nick thrust hard within her. She received him and returned his forceful passion with equal intensity, all sensation centered in the connection between them. When she felt his entire body shudder with release, she, too, relinquished control. The first spasmodic pulsations gripped her so strongly that her head and shoulders curled up from the bed, her face pressed against Nick's hot, moist skin, her teeth biting into his flesh to keep from screaming out her pleasure. She sank back down. Waves of feeling rippled through her like the aftershocks of an earthquake.

Nick rolled onto his side with his arms still around her. She rested in his embrace, wondering nervously as consciousness returned, who would speak first and what would be said.

"Susan."

He remembered her name, she thought giddily. That was a promising beginning.

With a soft puff of breath, he blew aside the hair clinging damply to her forehead and kissed her temple. "I have opened my heart wide and folded within the wet wings of my dove," he said.

"Ah, Elizabeth Barrett Browning." She nestled with satisfaction against him. "No one has ever called me a dove before." She leaned her head back in the crook of his arm in order to see him better. "If I'm a dove, what are you?"

He grinned. "A cock, of course. Do you need to be reminded so soon?"

She clucked her tongue at him in mock reproach. "No, a common rooster is entirely too domesticated for the likes of you." She ran her finger along the rakish scar cutting through his eyebrow and across his forehead. "What am I then?"

"A catbird. A wildcat, a tomcat, a polecat, a cat-o'-nine-tails, a cataclysm, a catastrophe." Her tongue followed the line her finger had just sketched.

Nick's breath quickened as he felt desire flood back at her touch. "Susan," he groaned, even less patient now than before. He pulled her on top of him and she bent willingly over him. He tried to speak, to tell her something before he was lost to words and speech, but she cut him off with her kisses.

At first Susan thought the loud pulsing she was hearing was merely the pounding of her heart, but gradually she became aware that the sound was coming from the phone on the nightstand. She raised her head and looked at Nick. "The phone is ringing," she said stupidly.

"Leave it. It's probably a wrong number." He drew her head down again.

"At two-thirty in the morning?"

Nick sighed and let his hands fall to his side. The phone kept ringing beside the bed.

"Maybe it's my mother. She has heart trouble." Her voice was scared as she remembered the long nights she'd lain awake when her mother had been in the hospital. She still did not quite trust the fact that her mother seemed to be well now. She rolled over to answer the phone, wrapping a sheet around her. "Hello?"

"Susan," a man said shakily, "there's been an accident. We were driving home and a drunk driver crossed over the center meridian and headed right toward us. I swerved to miss him, but he hit us anyway and the car was totaled."

For a minute, Susan was too paralyzed with shock to recognize the voice but in the silence, broken only by the man's ragged breathing, she finally gathered her wits together. "Richard? Richard, are you all right?"

"Michelle was thrown out of the car and I don't know... They won't let me see her."

"Richard, are you all right?"

"Yes," he managed to say, "they've looked me over in the emergency room and told me I can go home. I want to stay and see Michelle, but the doctors won't let me see her. They told me to go home and come back tomorrow. I don't know what to do." He started crying.

"I'll come get you. Where are you?"

"It happened so fast."

"Where are you?" she repeated patiently. After he told her, she said, "I'll be there in twenty minutes, okay? Don't go anywhere. Wait for me, okay?" When she got a coherent answer from him, she hung up the phone and started pulling clothes out of her dresser drawer. "I've got to go," she said to Nick over her shoulder as she slammed one drawer shut and jerked open another. "Richard has been in an accident." She clutched the bundle of clothes in front of her and headed for the bathroom to change. At the bedroom door, she paused and looked back to where he lay naked on the bed, still aroused from their abruptly interrupted lovemaking. "I'm sorry," she said haltingly. "I have to go and I don't know when I'll be back. When you leave, go out the back door. It will lock behind you." He didn't look at her, so she left the room without another word. What else was there to say?

All the way to the hospital, she mentally argued with him. *Look, I can't abandon my friends when they need me just because I've found a man who drives me crazy in bed.* Her skin tingled, imprinted with the memory of his touch. *Would you look away and not speak if it was Molly in trouble? It's no different. I have known Richard for five years. I've only known you for a week or so. What do I know about you?*

Richard was waiting for her just inside the emergency room door. His new suit was rumpled and torn. Wordlessly Susan took him in her arms and comforted him like she might comfort a child. "They won't let me see her," he said in a muffled voice.

"You told me." She patted him on the back and looked around for an attendant. When she saw a doctor walking down the corridor, a stethoscope hanging around her neck, she let go of Richard and hurried after her. "Excuse me, Doctor," she called. The doctor turned and waited for her to catch up. "I came to pick up Richard Temple. Did you examine him?" The woman nodded. "Is it really all right for him to go home? He says so, but he seems very shaky to me."

"Mr. Temple received minor cuts and abrasions in the accident but other than being stiff and sore for a few days, he should be all right. Someone should probably stay with him tonight, though, and keep an eye on him. He's had a bad shock."

"I will." She quickly repressed an image of Nick waiting in bed for her at home.

"I'll give him something to help him sleep."

"He is very upset about his companion, Michelle Easton. Can you tell me how she is?"

The doctor frowned. "She is listed in critical condition. We'll know more about the extent of her injuries tomorrow."

"Would it be possible for Richard to look in at her now? I think it would ease his mind if he could just reassure himself that everything possible was being done to help her."

"Believe me," the doctor said grimly, "the sight of Michelle Easton would do nothing to ease his mind. You know that she was thrown out of the car in the accident? No, take Mr. Temple home to get some rest. He'll be better equipped to face the facts in the morning."

It was nearly dawn by the time Susan got Richard home and settled down. She sat by his bed, holding his hand as he mumbled himself to sleep. The sun's first rays crept rosily over the windowsill, down the wall, and along the floor toward her until she was bathed in fresh morning light. Autumn had not yet sapped the sun of all its summer strength, but Susan was not warmed by its bright rays. She sat there, shaking with cold, thinking of Michelle lying in the hospital, her face swathed in thick white bandages, of Richard tossing and turning on the bed beside her, and of Nick. Where was he on this glorious fall morning that made such a mockery of human passion and pain?

NICK WAITED FOR SUSAN for hours, those long hours in the middle of the night that stretch out interminably, hours weighed down with uneasy thoughts, regrets, and futile speculation. Twice he dozed off and awakened with a start, thinking he had heard her key turn in the front door or that the phone had rung. But no footsteps sounded on the stairs and when he picked up the phone, the dial tone mocked his hopeful hello. At dawn, he gave up.

His clothes were crumpled in a corner of the room. He retrieved them and got dressed, indifferent to the wrinkles and faint traces of dust on his suit. At the doorway, he turned and walked back to make the bed. The pillows were pushed up against the antique wooden headboard, the quilt lay on the floor, and the top sheet, which had pulled free from the foot of the bed, was twisted and coiled like a satin rope. No woman had ever pulled away from him in the middle of lovemaking to run to another man. Let her come home to a pristine bed; let her crawl between the cold smooth sheets and wonder if she had merely dreamed the heat they had generated together.

He yanked the sheet off the bed and the roses she had worn in her hair fell out of the folds. Abruptly he sat down, sapped by the sight of the roses, now limp and bedraggled, but more fragrant than ever. He picked them up and the bruised petals scented his hands. Savagely he crushed the flowers and strewed the bed with rose petals until it looked like the rose-covered path a bride trods on her way to the altar or a grave still covered with funeral flowers. Leave the bed rumpled. He couldn't forget. Why should she?

6

SUSAN FINALLY GOT HOME at three o'clock the following afternoon. She had stayed with Richard until he woke up around noon and then had driven him back to the hospital. Michelle had regained consciousness and the doctors upgraded her condition, but this time it was Michelle who refused to see him.

"But why?" a bewildered Richard asked.

"I don't know," the nurse on duty replied, "but if that's what she wants, that's what she gets. She is in no condition to be upset."

"She thinks I'm to blame for the accident," he mourned in the car on the way back to his apartment. "That's why she won't see me." His eyes darted back and forth, monitoring the traffic all around them.

"I'm sure she doesn't," Susan said.

A car a block ahead of them started to slow down. "Watch out! That car is turning!" Richard's foot slammed an imaginary brake to the floor.

"I see it." She glanced worriedly in his direction. She was going to have to keep an eye on him for a while.

By the time she soothed Richard's fears, dropped him off, and drove home, she was exhausted. Smothering a yawn, she picked up the four-inch-thick Sunday paper on the front steps and stepped inside the porch. A single wilted rose petal lay on the floor. All traces of sleepiness vanished. What if Nick was still there? She didn't think she could face him in broad daylight, not after last night. What had possessed her to act like that, so aggressive, so shamelessly sexual? The answer came unbidden to her mind. Nick had possessed her, that's what.

She unlocked the door and listened for any sounds of human movement. The refrigerator hummed in the kitchen but other than that, a deep silence filled her empty house. She crept up the stairs to the bedroom. The first thing she saw was the disheveled bed covered with rose petals. Like a fortune teller who predicts the future from tea leaves, she tried to decipher the significance of the roses, but she could not. There was no future for Nick and her.

With a determined set to her chin, she stripped the bed, carefully folding the bottom sheet so the roses wouldn't fall out. Downstairs, she opened the back door, stood on the steps, and shook the sheet out. The breeze billowed the sheet like a sail on a ship and rose petals fluttered through the air. She watched until the wind had hidden them among the crisp brown leaves carpeting the ground, then turned and went back into the house.

There was no time to sit around and think about Nick, she told herself; that was all over with and there was work to be done. She had lecture notes to review for tomorrow's classes and thirty Introduction to Sociology essay tests to grade. She sat down at her desk, full of resolution, but she was soon fast asleep, her head pillowed on her arm. When she awoke two hours later, her neck was so stiff that she couldn't straighten her head.

Lurching like the hunchback of Notre Dame down the hall and into the bedroom, she made up her bed and set the alarm. She would have to get up at an impossibly early hour to get some work done before she went to school. As she gingerly lay down on the edge of the bed, she couldn't help but remember the night before. Bodies moving with fluid grace, tumbling over the big bed like young puppies, full of life and spirited battle. She shook her head to clear her thoughts and winced as the pain shot down her spine.

She shut her eyes tightly, refusing to cry. Maybe Nick would call and tell her that he wanted to see her again. Maybe she wouldn't get a bill from Elizabeth Mason and she could pretend that their night together had been a promise of what was to come.

However, he did not call and the imposing bill from the talent agency appeared promptly in her mailbox. Its appearance effectively weaned her from her romantic fantasies. Emptying her bank account, she sent the payment and, to salvage her pride, included a fifty-dollar tip for Nicholas Taurage "for services rendered."

To make matters worse, all week she was forced to hear Nick's praises sung by every faculty member who had met him. The parade into her office began on Monday when Phillip Hunter dropped in with a book on Kabuki theater. "Next time you see Nick, give him this book for me, will you?"

Close on the heels of Phillip Hunter was Steve Birnbaum who regarded Nick as a kind of Petruchio who had tamed his shrew. He pumped her hand in fervent gratitude and told her that he only hoped that she and Nick would be as happy as he and Karen.

On Tuesday during lunch, President Turner stopped by the long table where she was sitting with eight other professors. "Susan," he said, placing a paternal hand on her shoulder to attract her attention, "I was very pleased to meet Nick Taurage at the Faculty Club the other night." The conversation continued uninterrupted at the opposite end of the table, but she knew that eight pairs of ears were straining to hear what the president was saying to her. "Melissa thinks very highly of him." Susan murmured a wordless acknowledgment. "We hope to see him again at other Humboldt functions," the president said with a smile.

When he had walked away, all pretense of conversation at the table ceased. "The official Humboldt seal of approval," pronounced a physics professor.

"'We hope to see him again at other Humboldt functions.' Susan, you're stuck with him now. You won't dare bring another man on campus. President Turner won't approve."

Susan squirmed uncomfortably in her chair.

"Look, she's blushing. I thought blushing went out with virginity in the sixties."

On Wednesday, she ran into Fred Harrison on her way to check her campus mail. "Susan, everyone is talking about you and Nick and your unfortunate affair with Richard seems to be forgotten. Just thought I would keep you posted."

The next day, Roger Perkins bounced into her office with a big grin on his face. "I wanted to thank you again for introducing me to Nick," he said. "He's already spoken to Jack Philby down at Roughwood Press about my book. Philby called and I have an appointment with him next week."

By Friday, Susan was thoroughly sick of hearing about Nicholas Taurage, especially since she spent most of her sleepless nights either thinking about him or trying not to think about him. She had just locked her office door and was on her way out when Molly stopped by. It was four-thirty in the afternoon and the third floor of Grantley Hall was deserted.

Molly's simple "How's it going?" was enough to set her off. "I'm sorry I ever hired Nick to come to the Faculty

Club party," she burst out. "He spends one single evening on campus and attracts more attention than I've gotten in the past five years."

"You're exaggerating," Molly comforted.

"No, I'm not. I've had a steady stream of visitors to my office this week, people who barely knew I existed before Nick, all of whom feel compelled to tell me what a perfect gem he is. Ha!" She was on a roll now. "He's little more than a high-priced gigolo!"

"Shhhh, keep your voice down," Molly said uneasily, glancing up and down the corridor although there was no one in sight. "Look, why don't you come home with me? I'm making enchiladas for dinner. Miguel and the kids will be delighted to see you. Come on, it will take your mind off Nick."

"I can't," Susan replied, calming down a little. "I promised Richard I would go with him to the hospital. Michelle still refuses to see him. He has camped out at the hospital day and night, hounding the staff until they get fed up and call me to come get him. I've had to run down there three times this week. He wants me to plead his case to Michelle."

"Let's hope she relents so you can get some rest."

"I still have thirty essay tests to grade and I promised my students I would have back to them last Monday," she said with a grimace. "Every time I sit down to work on them, my mind goes blank. I haven't gotten any work done this week."

They walked down the stairs together but just as they left the building, Susan slapped her hand to her forehead. "I forgot a book I need to read over the weekend. I'm going to run back up and get it. Go ahead if you're in a hurry."

"No, I'll wait."

Susan ran up the stairs, unlocked her office, and grabbed the book off the top of her desk. She did a double-take just to make sure that there was nothing else she needed and then closed the door behind her. As she turned to go, the office door next to her opened and Will Lambert popped out. She jumped nervously. She had thought she had seen him go home earlier in the day and hadn't expected him to be still lurking around.

"Hi, Will," she said politely despite the strain she always felt around him. "Have a good weekend."

"You, too," he answered with a leer.

She controlled the shudder that ran through her at the sight of the big smirk on his face. He often made her uneasy but tonight he seemed creepier than usual. Resolutely, she put him out of her mind and hurried to join Molly.

BY THE MIDDLE OF THE NEXT WEEK, Susan knew something had gone wrong. At first, she was oblivious to the giggles and the conversations that stopped as soon as she walked into the room, but eventually she could not ignore the fact that people were openly staring at her. When Fred Harrison cut her dead in the corridor in front of a half dozen other faculty, she sought out Molly in her office.

"What is going on?" she demanded anxiously.

Molly's normally ruddy face was ashen. "You're not going to want to hear this. I just heard from Roger Perkins that people are talking about you and Nick." She paused as if reluctant to continue.

"What are they saying?" Susan forced herself to ask.

"It varies."

"Varies along what lines?"

"One story is that you hired Nick to be your date."

Susan sat down. "And?"

"Another story is that Nick is a male prostitute."

Her head began to hurt. It can't get any worse, she told herself in a feeble attempt at comfort.

"The most extreme story is that . . ."

"You mean, there's more?"

Molly nodded miserably. "The worst story is that Nick is a male prostitute and pornography star and that you and he are part of a big sex ring and," she finished in a rush, "that the two of you tried to recruit President and Mrs. Turner."

Susan stared numbly at her.

"Nobody really believes that last one," Molly hastened to tell her.

"Even the first version is utter disaster! How could anybody know I hired Nick?" Susan asked in a bewildered voice.

"I swear I haven't told a solitary soul, not even Miguel. I wanted to, but I didn't."

Susan managed a weak smile. "I wasn't thinking of you."

"You don't think Nick told?"

"No one else knows."

"But he thought you hired him for a social psychology experiment. That doesn't really account for the sex part of the rumors."

Susan swallowed the wrong way and coughed until tears came to her eyes. "Maybe he figured the experiment was a sham. He's clever enough," she said in a rough voice. "Maybe he wanted revenge."

"Revenge for what?"

Susan shrugged her shoulders. There was no way she was going to tell Molly about their incredible night together so abruptly ended by Richard's call for help.

Molly would never believe her. She had a hard time believing it herself! "It doesn't matter. The damage is done."

"At this rate, you're not going to have a chance of getting tenure. I helped you get into this, I'll help you get out of it," Molly declared. "It seems to me that you've got to hire Nick again. People have to get used to seeing the two of you together. Once they start to think of you as a couple, they'll forget all this nonsense. I'm speaking as a married woman here," she added with a grimace.

"Hiring Nick again is out of the question."

"Why?"

"For one thing, I can't afford it. For another thing, you're forgetting that, in all likelihood, he is the one who started the rumors."

"You know, I just can't see Nick doing a thing like that. Why would he?"

"Drop it, Molly," Susan said in a carefully controlled tone.

"All right, then we'll come up with something else. We'll fall back on the experiment story."

"No." Susan was adamant. "That would be worse. Don't you see? Any explanation I offer will be immediately suspect and I won't give lame excuses. I'd rather be seen as wicked than weak." She shook her head. "Or stupid, which is probably more accurate. I should have never mistaken Richard's friendship for love. I should have never listened to Fred Harrison. I should have never hired Nick." I should have never gone to bed with him, she mentally added to the list, but even as she thought it, she knew that the absolute truth was that she didn't regret it, no matter what the consequences. "What have I gained from all these schemes anyway?"

"Well, you're certainly visible now," Molly offered inanely.

"Oh, yes, I'm certainly visible!"

NICK WANDERED THROUGH the house inspecting his handiwork. In another couple of weeks, he would be through with this one. He already had a buyer lined up. It was satisfying to see the finished project but toward the end, he found himself losing interest in the house. The part he liked best was starting from scratch, tearing down the garish wallpaper the previous owners put up and pulling all the old threadbare electrical wiring out of the walls like a surgeon stripping varicose veins. This house had been particularly difficult to finish because he couldn't keep his mind on the job. He had started to phone Susan a dozen times since the Faculty Club dance but each time, he hung up. Dammit, she had ordered him around like a navvy. He was not at her beck and call. He had waited for her; now she could wait for him.

When he went back to his own house for lunch, he found a parcel from the University of Chicago Press and a letter from the Elizabeth Mason Agency in the mail. He set the letter aside and cut through the nylon strapping on the package with his Swiss army knife. He had ordered Susan's book, *Men and Women at Work*, after the audition and had been waiting for it ever since. The cover showed a man and woman wearing business suits and hard hats. He opened the book and read the acknowledgements. She ran through the list of her graduate school professors and concluded with her more recent connections. "I am especially indebted to Richard Temple, Associate Professor of Psychology at Humboldt College. He acted as a sounding board for most of my ideas without once sounding bored, a feat that surely attests to his forbearance and friendship as much as to his interest in the subject matter." Nick snapped the book shut. Very cozy, this friendship between Susan and Richard, he thought savagely.

He picked up the letter from Elizabeth Mason and ripped it open with his finger. The sharp edge of the envelope sliced through his skin and immediately a thin line of blood seeped to the surface. He swore and pulled out a check and a note from Elizabeth.

Dear Nickie,
Here is the check for your Humboldt performance. I must admit I was a bit worried about whether you would be nice, but Dr. Harkness must have been pleased with you because she enclosed an extra fifty dollars marked "for services rendered." I should have known I could trust you.

Love,
Elizabeth

Two seconds later, he was on the phone. "Lizzie, I want you to send the money back."

"What on earth for?"

"Just do it. I'll send you a check for the commission the agency would have received."

"Don't be ridiculous," Elizabeth said. "I'm not that hard up. What happened?"

"I'd rather not talk about it."

"Nick, I have to know if it is going to affect the agency."

"It won't, I promise you. This is just something between Susan and me."

"But what shall I say to Dr. Harkness when I return the money?"

"Tell her that I sometimes donate my time to needy causes."

"Are you sure?"

"Yes." His voice was implacable.

"All right," she said reluctantly. "I'll get it in the mail this afternoon."

"Thanks." Nick rang off. There was no point in going back to the other house. The finishing work that remained needed a fine, steady hand and he was in no mood to be delicate. He drove to the gym and worked out until the sweat trickled down his back. But he was no closer to forgetting Susan.

A few days later, when he was working at the Literacy Center, supervising a reading group of adult Hmong refugees, Melissa Turner peeked around the corner. She caught his attention and as soon as there was a pause in the class, said, "Nick, when you're done with this, will you come see me? It's important." He nodded and continued the lesson.

He had been avoiding her for the past several weeks, ever since the Faculty Club party. He knew she would pepper him with questions about Susan if she could catch him alone so he had taken care to be constantly surrounded with students or staff members. Melissa had an unfortunate habit of asking blunt questions. It looked as though there would be no escape this time. He didn't know what he would say if forthright Melissa asked him if he was in love with Susan. He hadn't been out with another woman since the night they had spent together. Was that love? When he saw a morning dove, he thought of her. When he saw someone wearing cords, he thought of her. When he passed a florist and there were roses in the window, he thought of her. Was that love?

She had taken possession of his heart and mind. There was nothing coy about her like the other women he had known. He was tired of being manipulated under the guise of flirtation. Susan was both straightforward and refreshingly awkward at times. She was quite truly herself, not artifice disguised as natural. And, for a few precious moments, he sensed that she shared his sense of the ridiculous, a feeling so intimate that it scared him even as it tantalized him.

After class, he made his way to Melissa's office with about as much enthusiasm as a misbehaving schoolboy called to the principal's office.

"Come in and please close the door behind you," Melissa said when he knocked on her open office door.

Nick sat down in the chair facing her desk. He had never seen her look so serious. This was not going to be the teasing inquisition he had expected.

"This is very awkward, but I felt we should talk about the rumors about you and Susan."

"What rumors?" Nick asked blankly.

"Susan hasn't told you?"

"No, she hasn't." He didn't know why he was still covering for her but he added, "I haven't had a chance to see her since then. I've been busy finishing up a house. What kind of rumors?" Susan's colleagues must have found out about her experiment. He had told Elizabeth that the experiment might backfire if the other professors found out about it and now it appeared that he was right.

"Oh, I hate this!"

Nick wondered why she was so agitated. He hadn't approved of Susan's experiment, either, but surely, now that people knew about it, she would drop it and there would be no real harm done.

"The rumor is that Susan hired you to come to the Faculty Club dance with her and—" she gulped "—that you are a male prostitute or pornography star, depending on which version one hears."

"What?" Had Susan talked about their night together? The possibility of her betrayal raked through him, slashing open old wounds.

"There's wild talk of sex rings and recruiting attempts on campus..." Melissa trailed off at the sight of his clenched fists, then screwed up her courage to go on. "And poor Susan! Did you know she was up for tenure in the spring?"

He didn't know. On the other hand, he really wasn't too interested in Susan Harkness's career at the moment.

"With all these rumors circulating, she'll be lucky to finish out the year, let alone get tenure."

"Perhaps she deserves what she gets," he said curtly.

"Why?" Her soft brown eyes darkened as she understood the reason for Nick's anger. "You don't think Susan started the rumors? Oh, no, Nick. You sound angry with her. Have you had a fight? Even so, she wouldn't have done it. That would be suicidal."

Nick's anger cooled as he listened to Melissa. She made sense after all. Susan had nothing to gain by talking. And as for him, what did he care what a handful of professors at Humboldt College said about him? He had nothing to lose. At any other time, he would have been amused by the gossip, perhaps even played along for the hell of it. It seemed he was losing his light touch.

"You know what a rough time Susan has had the past few years—her father dying of cancer..."

No, he didn't know that.

"Then her mother hospitalized soon after."

He didn't know that, either.

"And now this scandal! I can't imagine how she gets through the day, trying to carry on as usual, all the time aware that everyone is laughing at her, aware that someone hates her enough to ruin her."

Now that was something he did know about. He pictured Susan alone in her empty house, in her empty bed, and deeply regretted the torn roses, his silence, and the "needy causes." "What can I do?" he asked.

"I honestly don't know. I don't suppose we should do anything until we consult with Susan." Nick immediately reached for the phone on Melissa's desk, but she stopped him. "She's probably in class right now. Call her at home this evening."

Nick did a lot of thinking while he watched the clock for the rest of the day. He kept comparing Pamela and Susan, shifting them back and forth in his mind like a police artist trying to put together a composite sketch of a suspect from an Identikit. At first glance, they seemed an easy match—young, bright, ambitious professors—but once he got past that similarity, none of the pieces fit. The most telling difference between them was how they had reacted in bed.

Pamela had wanted a skilled lover, a technician. When he was with her, he had learned to hold back sexually. Now he realized that in doing so, he had also been forced to hold back emotionally and that reserve was probably what had saved him in the long painful months that followed. But Susan had not wanted sex carefully monitored and regulated. She had wanted passion stripped of its civilized veneer and he had given it to her. He tensed as he remembered the feel of her body at once submissive and rebellious beneath his. He wanted her still. What had he been waiting for? Funny how your priorities suddenly become crystal clear when someone you love is threatened. *Someone you love.*

THE PHONE RANG over and over while Susan debated answering it. It could be her mother or Molly or Richard, or it could be another obscene phone call. She had started getting them at all hours of the night ever since the rumors had spread around campus. She would answer and the person on the other end would whisper a sexual insult in her ear before she could hang up.

The constant ringing got on her nerves. She might as well answer it as sit there imagining the worst. "Hello," she said cautiously.

"Susan, it's Nick."

She gasped and, without thinking, immediately slammed down the receiver, jerking her hand away from the phone as if she had just been burned. Nick! She had given up hoping he would call and now he was the last person in the world she wanted to talk to. Elizabeth Mason's letter had arrived with her returned check that afternoon. When the phone rang again, she unplugged it.

A half hour later, he pounded on her door. "Susan, I want to talk to you," he shouted and continued to pound.

She didn't move from her desk but through the study window, she could see her neighbor's curtains twitching. If she didn't go down to talk to him, in another minute her neighbor would be dialing 911. She didn't need police cars, sirens howling, red lights flashing, pulling up in front of her house to add to her reputation.

She went downstairs and talked to him through the window in the front door. "What do you want?"

"Let me in. I want to talk to you."

"No."

He pressed against the glass, feeling like a convict in prison on visiting day. "Melissa Turner told me about the rumors going around campus. Why don't you explain about the experiment?"

"There was no experiment," she said in a flat voice.

A pause. "Then why did you . . . ?"

"I'm a needy cause," she retorted, eyes flashing. "I needed a date for the dance. I didn't know anyone suitable to ask, so I lied to Elizabeth Mason and hired you. Now you know the truth. Go away and leave me alone." She turned her back on him and walked up the stairs, leaving him standing on the porch, staring through the window after her.

Nick went home, nonplussed by her revelation. Her latest explanation left even more unexplained than the first story. Why had she needed a date for the dance so badly? Why had she gone to bed with him? What did Richard mean to her? If she hadn't started the rumors, who had and why? He had to talk to her again.

However, Susan refused to see him. She stopped answering the phone altogether and he found the roses he sent daily frozen in their boxes on her porch. Her resistance infuriated him. He wanted to help her, dammit! The more she repulsed him, the more determined he was to see her.

After a few days of frustrated attempts to talk to her again at home, Nick decided to confront her at Humboldt. He was reluctant to do it. He knew that his presence on campus would only add fresh fuel to the rumors already circulating like brushfire but she had left him no other choice.

SUSAN WAS IN HER OFFICE talking to a student about her research paper when she glanced up and saw Nick standing outside the open door. She froze; the words she had been about to utter about sample size and statistical reliability vanished from her lips. He smiled at her, a grim, determined smile, and then walked out of view. Had she just imagined him? Had he gone?

"Professor Harkness?"

Susan forced her attention back to her anxious student who was probably interpreting her stunned silence as disapproval. "Sorry, Jenny, I was distracted for a minute. Your proposal sounds fine. Why don't you write a rough draft of the questionnaire and bring it in? I can look it over and see if you need to change the wording of any of the questions or add more questions before you send it out."

As Jenny left, Susan's eyes remained fixed on the door but instead of Nick, another student, one of her advisees, poked his head in the door. "Can I talk to you about spring registration? It won't take long."

"Sure, come on in," she replied with an attempt at a smile.

"You have a lineup outside your office," the student informed her as he plopped down in the chair facing her desk and drew out his registration packet. "All I need is a signature," he said, handing her an official form. "I'm going to be studying abroad in the spring."

"Where are you going?" she asked as she signed the form.

"England," he said enthusiastically. He then proceeded to describe which classes he was going to take, where he was going to stay, and the side trips he was intending to take.

Ordinarily Susan would have loved to hear the details, but not today. She could barely stand the tension. Was Nick still there? Why? Was he going to make a scene? Add to the scandal?

Her student finally ran out of steam and stood up.

"If I don't see you before you go, have a great trip," she said.

He nodded happily and left her office whistling "Hail Britannia." For a brief moment, she thought of going after him and asking if she could go along. She needed an escape; she needed to get away from Humboldt College, gossip and Nicholas Taurage. Most especially, Nicholas Taurage.

The next student in the line in front of her office moved to the door but before he could step inside, a long strong arm blocked his way.

"I think it's *my* turn," Nick said to the student who took one look at his opponent's size and expression and quickly yielded.

Nick closed the door behind him and the office seemed to shrink in size. Susan felt light-headed, her breath coming in short gulps, her heart pounding in her chest. "What are you doing here?" she asked levelly despite her panic. "I told you that I don't want to see you."

He held up a hand to stem her objections. "I know you don't and," he added bitterly, "I'll sneak out the back way so no one else sees me, either." He paused and then looked at her, puzzlement, hurt and entreaty in his gaze. "Why are you treating me like this, Susan?"

"Look, I regret hiring you," she lied. She was going to talk about the alleged experiment and give him a scientific roundabout, but her composure broke down. "You told," she accused him in a shaky voice. "You started the rumors. How could you do that, Nick? After our night together. I know I ran out on you but I had no control over that. It wasn't my fault."

"I didn't tell anyone about...us," he denied. "I thought you must have talked because I certainly didn't."

He moved closer and she stood up and backed away a step. She didn't want him anywhere near her. She didn't trust him any more than she trusted herself.

"Anyway," he said softly, seductively, "that doesn't matter now. What are we going to do about us?"

She looked at him, astonished. "Us? There is no us."

"There could be." He moved a little closer. "There will be." She backed up a little farther.

"Nick, I really think you should go now. Things are just too messy to work out."

Instead of replying, he moved closer. She didn't think it was possible but her pulse accelerated so much that the individual heartbeats were indistinguishable; instead they came all in a heated rush. She retreated from his advance until she found herself stopped by the bookshelves lining the office wall. There was no more room for escape.

He bent toward her, his eyes mesmerizing, his body a temptation even now. He leaned closer still and, to her horror, she burst into tears. It was such a girlish thing to do that she hated herself even as she did it but she couldn't control her emotions any longer.

"Go away," she sobbed. "Please go away!" To her astonishment, Nick immediately backed off, his hands raised in front of him in defense.

"Don't cry, okay? I'm leaving. Just don't cry. I can't bear it. I didn't mean to make you cry."

Instead of stopping, she covered her face with her hands and let out all the grief and anxiety that had been pent-up for so long.

"Look, Susan, I'm going," he announced desperately as he moved toward the door. "I'm going now."

She didn't know why but that made her cry even harder.

He opened the door and stepped into the hall but before he walked away, he turned back to her. "There is an us," he said fiercely. "I'm not going to let you get away. I don't know how or when but somehow, sometime . . . sometime soon . . . I'll be back and you'll have to deal with me then."

NICK RELIED ON MELISSA, his mole on the Humboldt campus, for reports. They plotted together over coffee in Melissa's office at The Literacy Center. Susan no longer came to the Faculty Club, she told him. She had lost weight and looked terrible. She was applying for jobs at other universities. "You have to do something, Nick."

He was slouched in a bright orange molded plastic chair with his long legs stretched out in front of him and his arms folded tightly over his chest. "I've already tried everything I can think of," he said tiredly. Suddenly his face cleared and he sat bolt upright in the chair.

"What are you going to do?"

He waved her quiet. The idea had burst on him with the force of an August thunderstorm that sweeps through the hot humid city clearing the air and restoring tempers. Did he really want to go through with it? He would be risking public humiliation. Hadn't he had enough? A smile slowly formed on his lips. He had had enough of about everything but Susan. "I'm going to need your help," he said to Melissa. "You're going to have to talk to Ray. Here's what you say . . ."

THE DECEMBER FACULTY meeting was going to start in five minutes, but Susan continued to work in her office. A person passing by might first assume from the single-minded concentration with which she reached for one book, then another, as she stood in front of the floor-to-ceiling bookcase that she was searching for the final footnote citation for a manuscript that, once published, would at the very least change the course of sociology forever. A second look, however, would reveal that she was carefully lining up her books so that their spines were perfectly perpendicular to the shelf's edge.

She was interrupted by Richard who lounged against the door frame for a few minutes watching her before saying, "Do you think you can pull yourself away from your housekeeping long enough to go to the faculty meeting?"

"In a minute."

"Honestly, Susan, I don't see how you can think in here. It's so...so—" he searched for the right epithet "—so neat." Richard was notorious for having the messiest office on campus. "You never used to have everything alphabetized and cross-referenced. Leave the books alone and come on."

"I don't want to go."

"Why not? There's not much on the agenda. We should be out of there in an hour. I promised Michelle I'd be over by six o'clock." Michelle and Richard were seeing each other again since Susan had convinced Michelle that Richard was interested in more than her pretty face, which had been badly lacerated in the accident. Susan was genuinely pleased that they were back together but at times, Richard's chipper attitude wore thin, especially since she had never felt lower.

"Richard," she said, trying to control the note of exasperation that crept into her voice, "you know very well that everyone is sneering at me. I can't face them."

"You're not helping matters by hiding in your office. You might as well hang out a sign that says Fair Game—

Fire Away. You have to let them know that they can't hurt you because you don't care what they think."

"But I do care," Susan said with tears in her eyes, "and they can hurt me. They can deny me tenure. Richard, I don't want to leave Humboldt. What can I do?"

He handed her a tissue from the box she kept on her desk. "The only way to cut your losses now is to look them in the eye and laugh back. Now come on, the faculty meeting is about to start."

Susan knew he was right and summoning her nerve, followed him over to the administrative building. The lobby in front of the tiered lecture and concert hall where the faculty meetings were held was crowded. People were pouring coffee and helping themselves to the cookies that were laid out on a long wooden table just outside the door. Richard steered her in their direction.

"Steve, what's new in the chemistry department?" Richard reached around Steve Birnbaum to get cups.

"The saga of our battles with the maintenance crew continues." He started to turn around to tell the latest outrage but halted when he saw Susan hovering behind Richard. "Oh. Hello, Susan." He glanced at his watch. "Well, it's getting late. Better get into the meeting." He hastily poured himself a cup of coffee and took off to the lecture room although everyone else was still chatting in the lounge.

"See," Susan hissed to Richard. "I told you I was persona non grata. People either run away like I've got the plague or they get in so many sly insults at my expense and so clearly enjoy my predicament that I avoid them."

"Since when did you care what Steve Birnbaum thinks of you?" asked Richard with a shrug, ignoring the larger issue.

"He's on FTP." He had no snappy comeback for that one. "Never mind," she said, taking pity on his struggle to find something comforting or feisty to say. "Here, take your coffee and let's go in."

They sat in the top row at the back of the room and waited for the meeting to start. No one sat next to them.

The president banged his gavel on the podium trying to call the faculty to order. Between the president's pounding and half of the faculty loudly shushing the other half, it was several minutes before it was sufficiently quiet to begin the meeting.

The secretary read the minutes and Fred Harrison made his usual corrections. The minutes duly approved with corrections, the president stood up and said, "I would like to begin with an item that is not listed on the agenda. A guest has asked permission to address the faculty and after much consideration, I decided to let him speak. The circumstances are, I believe you will agree, unusual. Mr. Taurage?"

Nick entered from a side door at the front of the room. No actor had ever had a more dramatic entrance. He could feel the faculty snap to attention. "Thank you, President Turner." Thank you, Melissa. Together they had set the stage, but he was the one who had to play all the parts in the play—lover, conspirator, statesman and fool.

"I'm getting out of here," Susan whispered hoarsely to Richard as she groped for her purse on the floor.

He put a restraining hand on her arm. "You'll make it worse by going. You've got to stay."

Nick quickly scanned the room and located Susan. She looked so worn-out that he wanted to bound up the stairs, hug her and tell her everything was going to be all right. Then he saw Richard sitting next to her, his hand resting on her arm. Up to that moment, he had not been sure how far he was willing to go to be with Susan, but now he knew. He would not hold back.

With the patience of an adept orator, he took his time before speaking, nodding to the faculty he had met at the dinner dance, forcing them to acknowledge him. When he spoke, his voice was clear and confident. "Shakespeare said, 'Good name in man and woman, my dear lord, is the immediate jewel of their souls: who steals my purse steals trash; 'tis something, nothing; 'twas mine, 'tis his, and has been slave to thousands; but he that filches from me my good name robs me of that which not enriches him and makes me poor indeed.'" He paused and looked sharply at the faculty. "I am here to report a theft."

Everyone knew what he was talking about. Several of the worst offenders squirmed guiltily and started to worry about libel suits.

"I understand that there have been some scandalous rumors circulating on campus about Susan Harkness and me. I don't know who started these rumors or what they possibly had to gain by them."

A couple of people glanced surreptitiously at Will Lambert, sprawled arrogantly in his chair.

"I do know that Susan and I have suffered because of them and I want to put an end to them once and for all. My name is Nicholas Taurage, not Dr. Feelgood." A few chuckles greeted his remarks and he knew that he was going to be able to turn things around. "Susan is not my madame or paying customer. She is what you must have known her to be for the past five years—a professor who brings only credit to this college."

Susan stared down at her lap. She could not bring herself to look at Nick. Why was he here, defending her with such simplicity that her heart ached?

"Susan, this isn't the place or the time I would have chosen to ask you this question." A bitter note crept into his voice that even the most consummate actor could not have produced. "Gossip has robbed us not only of our good names but of our privacy. Will you marry me?"

She did look at him then.

"I first asked you to marry me at the Faculty Club dance. You thought I was joking and perhaps I was then, but I'm asking you again now and this time I'm serious." Indeed, there was no amusement dancing across his face to taunt her. He repeated the question. "Will you marry me?"

The only sound in the stunned silence that followed was the sound of seventy professors swiveling in their chairs to stare at Susan who froze like a young doe caught in the sudden harsh glare of a hunter's spotlight. Impossible to flee; he would follow her. Impossible to fight; she had no more fight left in her.

"Susan."

His voice was so soft and compelling that she was drawn to him once more despite herself. It would be wonderful to have someone to lean on, she thought wearily, and Nick was so big and strong. He didn't seem to feel the insults or hurt the way she did. He was offering her protection, a refuge, and she wanted it. But was this just a staged proposal?

"Susan?" His voice was more urgent this time and he held out his hand to her in appeal.

As she desperately tried to marshal her thoughts she realized that Nick had set it up so she couldn't lose either way. He was the one taking all the risk; he was the supplicant, she the arbiter. He had publicly abdicated his pride and his power. Why? Why would he do that for her? She didn't know, but she couldn't throw his offer back in his face. She could be as generous as he. "Yes, I will marry you," she said shakily.

Seventy heads swiveled back to Nick. His eyes glittered with triumph as he stepped forward. "Come here."

As she rose to her feet, Richard caught her arm. "Susan, are you sure you want to do this?" he asked in an undertone.

"Don't worry," she whispered back with more confidence than she felt. "I can handle it." She walked down the steps at the side of the room and was swept into Nick's arms.

He kissed her a brief hard kiss that set her nerves jangling with alarm and swung her around to face the faculty who applauded their congratulations. With his arm around her waist, he announced, "To celebrate our marriage, I plan to donate one million dollars to Humboldt College on our wedding day."

There was a stunned silence.

"All legitimately earned, I assure you," he added dryly.

Belatedly someone realized that they were being rude to a major financial donor and began another round of applause, which grew until it was even more enthusiastic than the first.

"And I intend all of it to go to faculty salaries."

This time the younger members of the faculty burst into some very undignified shouts and whistles.

"Maybe then you can pay me what I'm worth," Nick whispered to Susan as he pulled her closer.

"And what are you worth?" she asked in a dazed voice.

"Every penny," he replied with a mocking smile.

She started to tremble as the heat from the hand he had pressed against her stomach burned through the thin wool sweater she wore. She could handle it, she had told Richard. She could handle it. Already her body was betraying her. Already she was finding out that Nick was more powerful than she had ever dreamed.

Nick watched Richard shift nervously in his chair and then raise his hand like a timid student asking permission from the teacher to speak. He was going to protest, cause more embarrassment, perhaps even persuade Susan to change her mind. Nick stared scornfully at him, daring him to make a sound. Richard's hand slowly descended and he slumped in his chair.

Nick wasted no sympathy on his competitor. He wasn't finished with Susan yet. "Since I don't believe in long engagements," he continued in a pleasant voice, "the check should be in President Turner's hands by the first of the year." He felt her jump and held her tighter still.

The first of the year! she thought frantically. Tenure decisions weren't made until March. The first of the year! Today was the third of December. Too late, she realized that she had walked right into his trap. He was not offering her protection. He was the hunter!

7

SUSAN AND NICK WALKED through the cold December twilight back to her house. They had excused themselves from the rest of the faculty meeting, ostensibly to be alone, and alone they were. Silent, their breath puffing out empty white clouds against the cobalt-blue sky, they looked like comic-strip characters with nothing to say.

You've got what you want, Nick told himself. Give her time. But he knew he was not a patient man.

When they entered the porch, the first thing they saw were the florist boxes stacked in a corner like little white coffins. Susan hurriedly opened the door and went in. "Coffee?" she asked, piling hat, gloves, scarf and coat on a chair by the door.

He followed suit. "Yes, please."

She busied herself in the kitchen, heating water, grinding coffee beans, and letting the rich brown coffee slowly seep through the cone-shaped filter into the glass pot. She stretched out the ritual as long as she could, but at last they were seated at the card table, coffee mugs in hand, and she could no longer postpone speaking. "Suppose you tell me what's going on."

"I asked you to marry me and you accepted."

"I don't think it's quite that simple."

"It could be." A pause. "But you're not going to let it be, are you?" He looked at her closed face and sighed. "What do you want to know?"

"We already talked about this when you came to my office. I was very upset then and accused you of starting the rumors about me. That was probably unfair. I should have asked you first before jumping to conclusions. So I'm asking you now and I want you to tell me the truth. Did you start the rumors about me?"

"About us, you mean?" he corrected. "It seems to me that I came off as badly in those rumors as you did."

"It's my career at stake, not yours. My livelihood. I don't have a million bucks to throw around like you apparently do. Where did you get that kind of money anyway? You were supposed to be a starving actor. An itinerant carpenter. An impoverished publisher."

"Did I miss something? Are you playing off a script I didn't receive? I didn't know I was supposed to be anything but myself."

"Who are you?"

"Dr. Feelgood?" he suggested hopefully. "No?" She was scowling at him. "A pity. I am an actor, carpenter and publisher. I'm just not starving, itinerant, or impoverished. The money came from my family's men's clothing store business, which I built up and sold to Brooks Brothers seven years ago. Revel's. Perhaps you've heard of it."

Who hadn't? Some of her colleagues who did corporate consulting shopped there. Wonderful clothes but prohibitively expensive. "Why didn't you tell me about this before?"

"You never asked, thank God. You're not one of those women who check out a man's bank statement before they go to bed with him. *Au contraire*, my dear. You seem to favor the poverty-stricken artist. Why is that? Perhaps you are more romantic than you let on. Should

I give away the rest of my money? Dress in black? Grow a beard? Wear a beret?"

"And the rumors?" she persisted, trying to ignore his nonsense.

"I told you before, I did not tell anyone anything about us," he replied, sobered by the question. "Can you say the same?"

"Yes," she answered indignantly. Molly didn't count, she added to herself as an afterthought.

"When I mentioned the rumors at the faculty meeting," Nick said slowly, recalling the moment, "a number of people looked at a young guy sitting two rows from the front on the right-hand side of the room. He was wearing jeans and a blue sweater. Tall and thin, almost white hair, narrow-set blue eyes. Could he have anything to do with this?"

"Will Lambert," she exclaimed with a grimace. "Well, he certainly has the motive. He's been angling for my job all fall. But I never talk to him about anything except Humboldt business."

"The Faculty Club dinner was Humboldt business. Maybe you said something inadvertently and he put two and two together."

"No," she insisted. "I can't stand the man and I don't do idle chat with him. I may tell him that a student was looking for him or give him some mail that was delivered to my office by mistake but other than that, I avoid him. And it's not that easy to do because he's in the office right next to mine." She paused, something nagging at her memory.

"If it wasn't him, who could it be?" Nick asked. "I think we should sort this out. Otherwise we'll be wondering about each other for the rest of our lives."

But Susan wasn't listening to him. What was it that she was trying to remember? Something to do with Will Lambert. She pictured him, recreated him in her mind's eye, heard him laughing in that high-pitched laugh of his that was almost a whinny. Her eyes widened with shock.

"What is it?"

She clutched his arm. "The phone calls," she said breathlessly.

"What are you talking about?"

She explained to him about the harassing calls she had been getting until she stopped answering her phone. "I thought the man's voice sounded familiar but I couldn't quite place him before. Now I can. It's Will!"

Nick swore fiercely under his breath. "What kind of a man would do that?"

"A jerk," she said, drumming her fingertips against the table in repressed fury.

"If he made those phone calls, he'd also spread rumors."

"But how did he know?"

"Know about which part?" Nick asked dryly. "The hired part or the sex orgy part?"

"Either," she replied, and knew that a blush was tingeing her cheeks pink. Trying to still the feelings the mention of her night with Nick stirred up, she tried to remember any conversation with Will Lambert. All of a sudden, she remembered running into Will right after she had spouted off to Molly about Nick. She put her hand over her mouth in dismay. Will Lambert not only had the motive; he had the opportunity! Politics again. It was all politics.

"What is it?"

"I may owe you an apology," she mumbled, avoiding his eyes. "He may have inadvertently overhead something I said. . . ."

"Just what did you say?" He cupped her chin in his hand and forced her to look at him. "Forget it," he said when he saw how upset she was. What was the use of rehashing the past when they had the future to look forward to? "We've put a stop to the rumors. It doesn't matter anymore who started what or what was said."

But it did matter, she thought. It changed everything. "Why did you ask me to marry you? If it was my own fault the rumors started, there was no need for you to be so noble."

He laughed out loud at that. "I'm not being noble. Quite the reverse. I'm being extremely selfish. I won't let you put me off any longer. I want you on my doorstep all tied up with a bow."

"Neanderthal!"

"I don't think they gift-wrapped in the Paleolithic period." He grinned.

She repressed a smile, but couldn't resist joining in. "True, a bop on the head with an old bone and off to the caves was probably more like it."

"Whatever works."

She forced herself back to the issue at hand. "At any rate," she resumed sternly, "I can't do it. It's too irresponsible."

"You said you'd marry me in front of seventy witnesses."

"Temporary insanity, a moment of weakness."

"I wish you'd have more weak moments."

"You can wish all you like but it's not going to get you anywhere with me," she flung back. "I'll tell everyone we broke off our engagement and I'll just take my chances with tenure."

"And *maybe* you'll get tenure." He stressed the maybe. "But if your colleagues are as broke as you are," he wiggled her wobbly card table, slopping coffee over the edges of the mugs to illustrate his point, "they are going to be awfully disappointed they didn't get that pay raise. Every time they struggle to get their bills paid on time, every time another professor leaves academia for a better-paying job, they will think, 'If only Susan hadn't been so damn stubborn....'" In lieu of an old bone, he would bop her over the head with her good name, tenure, a million dollars, or anything else he could think of. Whatever worked.

"I should have known that the money had strings attached."

He threw her own words back into her face. "He who pays the piper calls the tune."

"You know," she said hotly, "this reminds me of an old joke. A beautiful young woman is sitting next to a wealthy old man at a charity banquet."

"Thanks a lot," Nick muttered.

"At the end of the banquet, he turns to her and says, 'Will you go to bed with me if I give a million dollars to this charity?' Of course, she doesn't want to go to bed with him, but the charity is a good cause, one might even say 'a needy cause,' so after thinking it over, she finally says, 'Yes, I guess I would.' 'Would you go to bed with me if I give you a dollar?' She slaps his face and says, 'What kind of girl do you think I am?' 'We've already established what kind of girl you are,' he replies. 'Now we're just haggling over the price.'"

Nick was not greatly amused. "Let me get this straight. You see yourself as the woman in that joke?"

"Yes."

"Oh, no," he said smoothly, "there's a difference, my charity girl, a big difference. You want to go to bed with me."

A denial sprung automatically to her lips, "No, I—"

"Liar, liar, pants on fire," he taunted, shaking his finger at her.

She couldn't help herself. The old childhood chant was so unexpected and unfortunately apt that she burst out laughing.

With a quick intake of breath, he reached for her.

"No, Nick, no!" Her eyes widened with panic and she backed away, the rubber feet of the folding chair squeaking a protest against the worn linoleum floor. If he touched her, she would give in without further thought or reason and this decision was too important to rush into unthinkingly. "We've got to talk."

He struggled to control himself. Her laughter had set the blood surging through his body with such primitive force that it took all of his will to calm down. "You want to know why I asked you to marry me. I'll tell you," he said at last. "I'm tired of flirtations that come so easily that I am bored with them in a few months. I'm thirty-four years old and I want to get married. I want one woman, a woman who challenges me, a woman I can spend the rest of my life with, and that woman is you."

"But why me?"

"Fishing for compliments?"

She reddened with embarrassment. "No, I need to know. I really don't know why."

She expected so little. Was that Richard's doing? he wondered angrily. "It's because you laugh at my jokes. I don't have to stop and explain everything. You always understand. It's because we drew sparks from each other in bed."

"Laughter and sex," she repeated dubiously. "Is that enough?"

"That's everything!" He hesitated before continuing. He had refused to parade his feelings before seventy spectators. Even now he was reluctant to use The Words. Words hardened emotions into heavy concrete blocks, stumbling blocks, cornerstones of prefabricated structures that he detested. His love was not like all the others. It was unique, intense, flamboyant, and playful.

But if she wouldn't let him convince her with his touch, which was so much more eloquent than any speech he could give, he must make do with words. "Susan, I am trying to tell you that I love you. I know it's sudden but believe me, it's true." He hunched his shoulders in frustration as he searched for the right words. The world's greatest poets had struggled for centuries to speak of love. How could he compete with their eloquence? "Somehow I recognized you the first time we met, even though we had never seen each other before. It was a deep, silent recognition that has grown in strength and certainty since then. I know I'm rushing you but there's no point in waiting. I know this is right. So, I'm asking you again, will you marry me?"

If she hadn't believed his declaration, his eyes would have convinced her. The gold lights were mesmerizing, sparkling with fire, consuming her doubts. Her breath came quickly, in pace with the pulse of her heart. He loved her. Maybe his proposal wasn't a trap after all; maybe it was a voice singing in the wilderness.

Should she marry him? She couldn't imagine ever wanting another man and the thought of having Nick to come home to at night melted some of the icy layers around her heart deposited by her father's death. She couldn't reciprocate and tell him that she loved him. After her mistaken feelings for Richard, she didn't trust herself. She knew she could never come to see Nick as a dispassionate friend like Richard, but there were other just as misleading emotions like lust or loneliness. No, she couldn't tell him she loved him, but she couldn't turn him away, either.

"All right then," she said softly and immediately after wondered if she was doing the right thing for Nick's eyes blazed with such happiness that she was afraid. Was she being fair to him? "I'm worried that you'll be disappointed, Nick. You don't know what you're getting into if you expect me to be there for you, footloose and fancy-free. During the school year, I can't call my life my own. I won't have a lot of time for you."

He brushed off her warning. "People always make time for the things they care about most."

"That's what I thought I just said," she replied carefully.

"I see." The light in his eyes faded as her message sunk in.

Perversely, she felt bereft instead of satisfied that she had made her position perfectly clear.

"You know, it's dangerous to put so much of yourself into your work." His voice reverberated with a deep timbre as if he was speaking to her from across a vast distance of time and space, a prophet, a doomsayer. "Loneliness starts to gnaw away at your gut and you don't even know it until one day you wake up feeling hollow inside. You'll do anything to fill up that emptiness. You get reckless, take wild chances, make mistakes."

Goose bumps rose on her arms as he talked. "Maybe this marriage is one of those mistakes," she answered.

"For me. For you. If you want to change your mind, I'll understand."

"No," he said. "I don't want to change my mind." And I'm not going to give you time to change yours, either, he silently vowed.

They set the wedding for December 29, the day after Susan's fall semester final grades were due in the registrar's office. The wedding would be small, they agreed, just family and friends. "Molly and Miguel," Susan recited, jotting down the names of the guests on a yellow legal pad. "Richard, that makes three..." She paused, wondering if she should count Michelle, too. Would she be out of the hospital by then? Would she and Richard be on or off again?

"Three's a crowd."

The harsh note in Nick's voice startled her. "What is that supposed to mean?"

"I don't want him at our wedding."

"He's a friend of mine. If he's not invited, there will be no wedding."

So that's how it goes, he thought with a wrench but said nothing.

"You're asking Elizabeth Mason. She's a friend of yours," Susan pointed out more reasonably. "It's the same thing."

"No, it's not. Elizabeth is coming with her husband and children."

"I'm not going to drop Richard just because he's still single and I'm getting married. I couldn't respect myself if I dumped a friend like that and I don't see how you could respect me, either. You will just have to trust me." When he did not look particularly happy with this solution, she put her pen down. "Nick, maybe we're rushing into marriage too fast. There's so much we haven't talked out. Maybe we should call it off."

He caught her arm. "I know what you're doing," he said intensely. "Don't think you can put me off so easily. Richard be damned! Go ahead and invite him. Let him dance at our wedding!"

At times Susan didn't think she would survive the three weeks before the wedding. First, there was the awkward phone call to her mother. "Hi, Mom, guess what?"

"But this is so sudden," her mother said in a bewildered voice after Susan had told her the news. "Are you sure? Do you love him? Who is he?" Susan tried to reassure her over the phone, but she could sense her anxiety and that added to her own.

"I don't know what this will do to my mother's health," Susan worried. "We should have gone to visit her and broken the news to her more gently, but I just can't get away right now."

"Why don't I go to meet her on my own?" Nick suggested.

A week later, she received an ecstatic phone call from her mother. Nick had said this and Nick had done that. "Darling, I love him already. Such a wonderful man! I'm so happy for you. Now, about wedding arrangements..."

The pace picked up.

Then, two weeks before the wedding, there was the trial run at his widowed mother's house, complete with his four sisters and their families. She smiled until her face ached as she listened to the endless stories of Nick's childhood that her future sisters-in-law were convinced any doting bride-to-be would want to hear. Finally Nick ordered his sisters to stop boring everyone to tears and the conversation turned to less personal matters.

His mother was a quiet, self-assured woman who studied Susan intently when Nick introduced them. They didn't have a chance to speak until later in the evening. They were seated at the far side of the spacious living room, watching Nick. He and three of his nieces and nephews were playing amidst a rubble of building blocks, miniature cars, and mismatched tea sets.

"Do you love my son, Professor Harkness?" Amelia Taurage suddenly asked.

"Ah, ah, Susan," she stammered. "I wish you'd call me Susan."

"Do you love Nick?"

She had asked herself that question so many times without coming up with an answer that she had given up. She wanted to say yes, but she hesitated. She had been originally attracted to him because he was so strong and confident. She had wanted to take refuge in that strength, but now it was that very quality that made her hold back. She was like a tiny sailboat circling a giant whirlpool, irresistibly attracted but struggling to keep a safe distance. If she let go, what would be left of her?

The awkward silence, which was answer enough, was broken by the sound of Nick's deep laughter mingled with the childish trebles. "You might think to look at him that he has always had an easy life, but he has had his share of troubles. Has he ever talked to you about it?"

"No," Susan admitted, realizing with a sense of shame she had never asked him much about his life before he had met her. There was never enough time. "What troubles?"

Mrs. Taurage shrugged. "This is for him to say. I shouldn't have mentioned it, but I am concerned. Don't hurt my son, Susan."

"I'd never do anything to hurt Nick. I mean it. I do care about him."

"In the law, there are crimes of commission and crimes of omission," the older woman replied. "That holds true in marriage as well. If you remember that, Susan, you'll have my blessing."

After that, the pace picked up a little more.

She and Nick saw each other every day or evening but they were seldom alone. There was a holiday party at the Faculty Club, the end of classes, a day-long Christmas-present shopping blitz, another holiday party at the president's house, shopping for a wedding dress and final exam week with its stacks of grading coming in.

It was all fun but Susan fell into bed every night utterly exhausted and dreamed she and Nick were happily picknicking in a grassy field when all of a sudden, a stampeding herd of cattle bore down on them. Dishes went flying this way and that as their hooves churned up the turf. Nick made an effort to grab her, but they were separated by the panicked animals. She managed to keep on her feet and the herd split around her. Peering through the dust and galloping herd, searching for Nick, she called out his name. She could hear him calling her, too, but the cattle forced them farther and farther apart. She woke up more tired than before she had gone to sleep.

The days passed in a rush. Before she could stop and think, it was the day after Christmas and she was home in Wisconsin.

"Should we book hotel rooms for your out-of-town guests?" her mother was asking her. "I know most were planning to just drive from Minneapolis and go back the same day, but the weather forecast is for heavy wet snow. I'd hate to think of them getting stuck here with no place to stay. Susan, are you listening?"

"Yes, Mom, in a minute. I've just got to total these grades and I'll be done, okay?" She didn't look up from the grading sheets that were spread out on the kitchen table in front of her. Her fingers rapidly punched the numbers in on the calculator, arriving at a single total that summarized the months of reading, writing and thinking. She hated this part of the job.

Nick watched her as she fidgeted in the chair and rubbed her temples. She penciled in a grade for a student, erased it, changed it, erased it again, and changed it back to the original grade. "I'll call the hotel," he said. He got up and went into the living room to use the phone so he wouldn't disturb her.

A half hour later, grades finally completed, she found him, still sitting in the living room. "All done," she announced with a yawn. She stretched, trying to relieve the stiffness from hours of hunching over her work. "Now, what was Mom talking about? Something about booking hotels?"

"I took care of it."

"Thank you. You're being very sweet about this mess. I'm sorry my grading took so long. It's just that I had so many students this term."

"Come here," he patted the footstool in front of his chair. Wearily she obeyed, leaning back into his hands as he massaged her shoulders.

"You've been awfully quiet the past couple days," she ventured after a few moments. "Having second thoughts?"

He could feel the tension in her muscles. "No," he said. She relaxed a little, her flesh becoming more pliable to his touch.

"Then what's wrong?" She took a deep breath as he slid his hands from her shoulders down along her spine.

"Maybe I'm getting tired of waiting." They had not made love since their first night together. When Susan had proposed celibacy as a test of their relationship, he had agreed. Personally he thought sex was the best test, but if she was worried that it confused things, he could compromise. After all, he loved her out of bed as well as in it, but he was rapidly coming to the conclusion that if he had to maintain control much longer, he was going to flunk the test. His arms went around her waist and pulled her back against him in the chair. He reached around her, unbuttoned the top three buttons of her blouse, and slipped his hand inside her exposed lacy bra.

Susan struggled to her feet. "Mom could walk in here at any minute!"

"Then why don't we go to the hotel?"

"There's too much to do," she said, safely buttoned and seated four feet away from him. "I can't just desert Mom in the middle of all the wedding preparations." The telephone rang. She glanced at her watch. "That will be Richard calling from the office. He said he would turn my grades in for me. I'll get it in the kitchen."

Nick could hear her laughing and talking to Richard before she started to list off her students and their grades. Just one more day, he thought.

Susan was up the next day at dawn, running errands, coordinating music, flowers and food. Somehow their small, simple wedding had grown into a major production. Nick offered to help, but Susan's mother wouldn't let him into the house.

"You're not supposed to see the bride on the wedding day. It's bad luck," she told him as she sent him back to his hotel room to count the hours until the whole damn wedding business was out of the way and he could be alone with Susan for the first time in weeks. He paced up and down the room, imagining the night that lay before them.

The wedding went off with a hitch, or so Susan was told. Forever after, she could remember only bits and pieces, a few memories etched in sharp contrast to the general blur. Nick's eyes as he watched her walk down the aisle. The tears trickling down her mother's cheeks as she glanced at the empty place by her side when the minister asked, "Who gives this woman to be married to this man?" Nick's big hand confidently clasping her trembling one as he slid the narrow gold band onto her finger. Molly laughing and crying simultaneously until Miguel led her off to calm her down with cake and champagne. The look on Nick's face when Richard had hugged her in congratulations.

The snow held off until they were on their way to Nick's cabin in northern Minnesota. He put the car in four-wheel drive, and they plowed through the snow that slithered across the highway in hypnotizing waves and settled in massive drifts by farm places. At times they could see far ahead—farms lit up and dancing in the distance like fireflies, small towns with golden halos warming the dark, cold sky. Other times, they peered through the white landscape trying to keep on the road.

"Maybe we should turn back or stop at the next town." They had been driving for three hours and Susan's eyes ached from the blinding white snow.

"We're almost there. Another twenty minutes should do it. Hang on."

She gritted her teeth and literally hung on, as they turned off the main road and bounced along a winding gravel road lined with drooping pines, their dark green branches weighed down with wet snow. When they pulled in and came to a stop five feet away from the cabin, Susan nearly fell out of the car and kissed the ground. Nick came around to help her over the four-foot drift in front of the cabin door. "Whose bright idea was this?" she muttered as she stumbled on shaky legs through the snow.

"I take full responsibility," Nick said, "because later I mean to take full credit." He scooped Susan up in his arms and licked a snowflake off her cheek.

He unlocked the door and put her down inside, warming her cold lips with his mouth, but she just stood there, eyes closed, passively receiving his kisses without much response.

"I'm sorry," she murmured, sensing his disappointment. "I'm awfully tired." She tried to joke it off. "I vowed not to be an unimaginative wife who continually pleads tiredness or a headache, but here I am already. We must be well and truly married."

He kissed her gently on the temple. "Sit down and rest while I start a fire and bring in the suitcases from the car." He led her over to a deep plush couch by the stone fireplace, poured her a glass of brandy from the basic supplies he had brought up a few days before, and handed it to her before turning to the fireplace. Within minutes, a fire crackled and sparked in the hearth. "All set?" he asked.

She smiled gratefully at him and laid back against the couch pillows.

"I'll be right back," he promised and plunged into the storm. The wind blew sharp and strong across the frozen lake, carrying the faint subterranean sound of frigid blue water crystallizing into ice. He stood still for a minute, breathing in the fresh scent of pine, cedar and spruce, the snow stinging his face. Then, when the cold had penetrated the marrow of his bones, he thought of Susan waiting for him inside in the fire-flickering warmth. He wanted to throw back his head and howl at the hidden moon until the sky echoed with his fierce happiness.

He carried their bags into the bedroom and quickly unpacked. In a moment of feminine vanity, Susan had brought a transparent negligee totally unsuited for north woods winter wear. Its slinky fabric brushed coolly and seductively against Nick's fingers as he laid it out on the bed. Blood racing with impatience, he tossed the empty suitcases into the closet and went into the living room.

Susan was sound asleep on the couch where he had left her, still bundled up, still clutching the stem of her brandy snifter, which threatened to tip out its contents all over the braided wool rug in front of the couch. He sat down in a chair across from her, his excitement ebbing as he noticed the tired lines around her eyes and mouth. Her chest rose and fell with slow steady breaths. With a sigh, he got to his feet and rescued the glass. She was limp in his hands as he took her coat off and didn't even stir when he carried her into the bedroom and put her into bed still wearing her jeans and sweater. He didn't trust himself to undress her.

He gulped down the rest of her brandy and went back outside. Late into the night, the swirling sky echoed with the sounds of chopping wood as Nick worked his way through the woodpile, splintering mighty oaks into kindling.

When Susan awoke twelve hours later, Nick was lying by her side. Never had a couple spent such a chaste wedding night, she thought as she sat up in bed, she completely clothed under the quilt, he completely clothed on top of it, like New England sweethearts in bundling days. Poor Nick! It probably wasn't what he had in mind.

Cautiously she tiptoed out of the bedroom, carrying clean clothes with her, in search of a hot shower and a cup of coffee in that order. Nick was still sleeping soundly when she finished her coffee so she left him undisturbed, put on her cherry-red parka, and set out to explore the woods around the cabin.

It had stopped snowing sometime in the early-morning hours and she could see the sun, a cool white disk, suspended in a thin layer of gray clouds. She walked for an hour along the beach, gazing across the windswept lake to the shoreline on the other side. All the other cabins that she could see were boarded up. She and Nick apparently had the lake to themselves.

"Hey there, little Red Riding-Hood," a baritone voice sang out from behind a tree, "aren't you afraid of meeting up with the Big Bad Wolf?"

"Hello," she called in the general direction of the voice. There was no reply, only the sound of a twig snapping underfoot. "Nick?" Still no reply. "Nick!" She listened intently, her head cocked to one side. "Come out, come out, wherever you are." She waited a minute more and then took off through the woods. She ran fast, jumping over fallen tree trunks half-rotted into the ground, ducking under low-hanging branches, a red cardinal darting through the snowy woods. She could hear heavy feet pounding after her.

"Here comes the Big Bad Wolf," he shouted a little breathlessly, hot in pursuit.

Laughing and running, Susan glanced back over her shoulder to see how far ahead she was and nearly decapitated herself on an outstretched tree limb. As she skidded to a stop, her feet flew out from under her and she sailed under the bottom branches of a thick evergreen.

Her toboggan run sans toboggan came to an abrupt halt when she connected with an unyielding tree trunk.

Nick rounded the last clump of bushes that separated him from Susan. She should be right in front of him, within arm's reach, but there was no sign of her any-where. He couldn't hear her running, so she must be hiding close by. His eyes searched for a patch of red but all he could see were the muted greens and browns of the woods, the pure white of the snow. The scuffled snow. He followed her trail to the huge evergreen and dropped onto one knee to peer beneath the branches.

Susan was sitting cross-legged on the ground, leaning against the tree trunk, catching her breath. He crawled in to join her. The evergreen branches, laden with wet snow, brushed against the ground all around them, creating a fragrant green bower. They could look up and see the tree trunk shooting upward to its perfect peak and its branches arching outward, like exposed beams in a cathedral. The sheltered ground underneath the tree was carpeted with a bed of surprisingly soft rusty-colored needles.

"You've run straight into the wolf's lair," Nick said. The soft white light of the sun penetrated their hiding place and illuminated Susan's smiling face. He touched the locks of hair that had escaped her stocking cap and curled against her temple. Then he kissed her, gripping her shoulders with his gloved hands, pulling her with him as he sank back onto the cushioned ground.

She nuzzled his cheek, taking tiny nips at his ears.

"Entirely too many clothes." He tugged at his gloves with his teeth to free his hands.

"Nick, you can't want to . . . Here? Now? Don't you think it's a little too cold?"

"Yes! No!" He tightened his grip on her as she struggled to escape. "Damn these gloves!" He released her in order to rip them off. She scrambled to her hands and knees, but he caught her by the waist before she could crawl away. Bending over her, he reached underneath her to unbutton her coat and push up her sweater. His hand slid along her taut stomach to her full breasts. She swayed beneath him on her hands and knees, acquiescent, her resistance melted away by his touch. He unsnapped her jeans and pulled them down over her curved hips, down her slim white thighs.

With one arm still holding her by the waist, his breath hot against her ear, he unfastened his own jeans. "Wolves mate for life," he whispered huskily as he took her in the sun-dappled den in the woods.

8

"DO YOU WANT ANYMORE?" Susan asked Nick. She was standing in front of the stove, holding a ladle and a saucepan. "There's just a bit left." He shook his head. "Maybe I'll finish it up then." She poured the soup into her bowl and came back to the table to eat. "I was absolutely ravenous, weren't you?"

"Ravenous," he agreed, a smile lighting up his face.

She stopped midspoon. "Are we talking about the same thing?"

"Absolutely."

"I wonder why I don't believe you," she said mockingly and resumed eating.

He got up to put his dishes into the sink and dropped a kiss on the top of her head on his way by. "Because you're an intelligent woman who knows the difference between one appetite and another," he replied.

She smiled at him, utterly relaxed and content.

"You cooked. I'll do dishes."

"I'd hardly call it cooking. I opened a can. Here, let me help."

"No, go ensconce yourself on the couch in front of the fire."

Dutifully, Susan ensconced herself. An elegant word, she mused, for laying around doing nothing. She could hear Nick working in the kitchen, half singing, half humming some indistinguishable tune, accompanied by the sound of water taps turning on and off and glasses clinking together in the soapy water. Lulled by domesticity, her eyelids dropped lower and lower.

"Unless you're keen on seven-can casserole," he said when he came out of the kitchen, "we need to get more groceries."

She struggled to sit up, but her muscles didn't seem to want to obey her.

He came to the couch and sat down beside her. "Darling, you look too sleepy to budge an inch. Why don't you stay here and have a nap while I run into town?"

"Why are you being so nice?" she asked drowsily, tugging his shirt collar, pulling him down toward her.

"It's my nature."

"It's a plot," she said as she nuzzled his throat.

"You've found me out. Curses, I am undone."

"No, you're not," she teased lazily, running her finger down the fastened buttons on his shirt, down the zipper in his jeans, and laughing at the startled expression on his face.

"I soon will be if I don't leave immediately," he said, recovering his aplomb. "I'll be back in an hour or so."

She listened to the car drive off and settled down with a comfortable sigh, but with Nick gone, the silence rang out as loud as an alarm clock. Within five minutes, she was thoroughly awake.

Giving up on sleep, she got up to explore the old log cabin that Nick's grandfather had built. Nick had winterized it and added a modern bathroom and kitchen to the original four-room structure. Each of the two guest bedrooms had a double bed and a set of bunk beds to accommodate Nick's nieces and nephews if they chose to sleep inside rather than camp out on the beach. The closets were full of old sweatshirts, sticky card decks, five-hundred-piece puzzles with pieces missing, suntan lotion, and storybooks. A shed out back housed the lawn chairs, baseball bats, bikes, croquet set, fishing poles, and life jackets—all the debris of summer at the lake.

She should have gone in to town with Nick, she thought crossly, still restless after her prowling. Nothing to do but read a book. She hadn't brought anything with her, but the bookcase should yield something interesting. She crooked her head and started to read the titles and authors of the books that he had crammed onto his shelves. Fiction rubbed shoulders with plant and bird guides; poetry mingled with biography.

One book on the bottom shelf was shoved so far back that she couldn't read the title. She knelt down and pulled it out of the densely packed row. *Fumbling the Ball* by Pamela Whitbread. Nick's strange reaction to the discussion of *Fumbling the Ball* at the Faculty dinner dance flashed through her mind and she examined the book with uneasy curiosity. Its spine was broken as if it had been either read or hurtled against the wall many times.

Feeling like Bluebeard's wife, she opened the front cover. The author had inscribed: "For Nick, because I couldn't have written the book without him. Pamela." Susan's grip on the book tightened. He hadn't said anything about actually knowing Pamela Whitbread. She sat down and began to read.

NICK PARKED BEHIND THE CABIN and started to carry in the food, wine and roses that filled the back seat of the car. He had been forced to drive an extra twenty miles to the next biggest town to get the flowers, but he had wanted them for Susan. Arms loaded with packages, he managed to open the door and squeeze through without dropping anything. "I'm back," he announced, stomping the snow off his boots and peering over a big loaf of bread sticking out of a bakery bag.

Susan was sitting on the floor by the bookcase, an open book on her lap.

"What is it?" he asked when he saw the expression on her face.

She held up the book, which he recognized immediately. "Oh, that," he said. A heartbeat later, he continued on into the kitchen and started to mechanically unpack the groceries.

She followed him, still carrying the book. "It's about you, isn't it?" He didn't answer, but there was no need for him to confirm what she already knew. Pamela had described him from the scar on his temple right down to the birthmark on his thigh.

As she watched him put away the groceries, she leaned against the kitchen counter, thinking hard. She remembered Nick's mother referring to his share of troubles. This must be it. How horrible for him to be ridiculed so viciously, so publicly! How could Pamela Whitbread have done it? She was shocked at the rage that churned inside her at the thought of Pamela.

"I'd like to hear about it, if you want to tell me," she said hesitantly. She felt that they had already arrived at an important crossroads in their marriage. This was what marriage was all about, this delicate confrontation of hidden pain.

"It's history," he said gruffly. "No need to go into it."

What should she do? She had agreed to share this man's life, his past, present and future. And now, here was his past captured in stark black print on the white pages that trembled in her hands. She sensed that his future hung in the balance between the lines. Their future. "Please talk to me, Nick."

He looked into her concerned green eyes and suddenly wanted to share the burden made more burdensome for having to bear it alone. "All right," he said. But having decided to talk, he didn't know where to begin. He poured them both a cup of coffee and led her into the living room. After putting another log on the fire, he settled down on the couch beside her and stared at the fire for a long time before he could find the words.

"I led a charmed life until I was twenty. My family was not rich, but my father made a comfortable living running Revel's, although it was just one small store at that point. During the school year, I was too busy with homework and sports to do much in the store, but I used to work there all summer and learned a lot about the business. Being the only son, I was slated to take over when my father retired. However, he was a relatively young man and I didn't think that far ahead. I was a carefree kid." He fell silent, remembering.

Susan pictured him as a teenager. Unlike her, he would have escaped the moody agonies of adolescence. Not for him the awkward self-consciousness or the physical clumsiness. He would have glistened with rude good health and spirits, one of those shining stars that she had worshiped from afar in a corner of the library.

"My father unexpectedly died of a heart attack when I was in my sophomore year at the University of Minnesota. One minute I was playing football and studying nineteenth-century English literature and the next minute I was the head of the family and the business."

His voice was steady, the tone factual, but she understood about fathers dying. She reached over and took his hand. "Were you close to your dad?" she asked, curling her fingers around his in unspoken comfort.

"We were close when I was a kid, but we drifted apart as I got older. By then, I already knew that I didn't want to spend the rest of my life working at Revel's. He knew it, too, and it hurt him. After he died, I tried to make it up to him by becoming what I thought he would have wanted me to be. I dropped out of college, and when I say dropped out, I mean dropped out. I stopped seeing college and high-school friends, stopped reading, stopped playing sports, stopped playing period. For the next six years, I did nothing but work. I was driven to provide for my mother and sisters and to make Revel's a success."

"You obviously succeeded."

"Yes, I did very well financially." But he didn't seem to take much pleasure in his success.

"Where does Pamela Whitbread come into it?"

"My youngest sister, Katie, was in her final year of college, majoring in English literature at Yale. Pamela was a teaching assistant in one of her courses. Katie worshiped the ground she walked on and when she learned that Pamela was going to be at loose ends for a few weeks before taking up a faculty position at Berkeley in the fall, she invited her to come visit us.

"At the time, I had just opened two new stores, which were already exceeding my original projections. My sisters were all settled into independent lives. For the first time in six years, I felt I could take it easy. I looked up from my balance sheets and there was Pamela Whitbread in all her glory. I fell hard and since she had nothing better to do—" bitterness crept into his voice "—she played along. We were constantly together during the time she spent in Minneapolis and after she left, I commuted back and forth between Minnesota and California for about a year.

"I hated commuting, seeing her once or twice a month, talking on the phone in between times. I was willing to move to California, but she put me off, saying that she wouldn't have any time to see me."

Susan squirmed remembering how she had told him the same thing.

"Besides teaching full-time, she was working on a novel. 'Maybe when the novel is done . . .' she told me. Later I realized that she kept me around for 'research purposes' because as soon as she was finished writing, she broke it off between us. I was too smitten to accept the terse 'Dear John' letter she sent, so I flew out, convinced I could change her mind if I could just talk to her in person. I was stunned by the transformation in her. She was cold and scathing, but I still believed that we were just having a lovers' quarrel. I came home and worked harder than ever to build up the business to a point where I could sell it and be free to move to California. I figured that we could work things out."

His grip on her hand tightened so much that she nearly cried out in pain.

"A fool and his innocence are soon parted. Six months later, I received *Fumbling the Ball* in the mail. When I read Pamela's inscription, I thought that this was at last a reconciliation move. I cancelled all my appointments for the afternoon and sat down to read."

Susan could imagine what was coming and wished desperately that he would stop. It shook her to see him suffering, but she said nothing, let him continue talking, helped shoulder some of the hurt.

"There I was as the main character, Rick, barely disguised. And my family! She turned all of us into a ridiculous caricature with just enough truth thrown in to be recognizable. Poor Katie was shattered. I'll never forgive Pamela for that." His face was hard, anger carved out of stone.

"I came up here to the cabin and read the book over and over, torturing myself with the details. I could recite you entire passages. For example, 'Rick was like a Mexican piñata. The outside packaging was alluring but inside was nothing but empty space, sickeningly sweet candy, and cheap toys.' Or, 'Having sex with Rick was an exercise in futility. Futility: something futile. Futile is applied to that which fails completely of the desired end or is incapable of producing any result; intrinsic inefficacy.' Or how about this one? It's a classic—"

"Stop it! Stop it," Susan said softly, pulling her hand free from his bone-crushing grasp so she could gently stroke his damp forehead and run her fingers through his thick black hair. She soothed him until his chest stopped heaving with emotion, his breathing calmed to a slow, steady rhythm, and he was able to continue.

"And then you came along, another female academic who wanted me for research purposes," he said in a wry voice. "I took on the job because I wanted to prove to myself that I was fully recovered. I was horrified when I found myself falling in love with you. I fought it, particularly after you went running off to another man in the middle of the night."

"Richard and I are just friends," Susan protested.

"So you keep saying," he replied cryptically. Maybe someday she would tell the truth as he was doing. Maybe someday she would love him enough to do that. "When I heard you were in trouble at Humboldt, I wanted to help, except, just like Pamela, you wouldn't talk to me. You didn't have time for me."

"If I'm so much like her, why did you marry me?" Susan was getting a bit nettled at the comparison.

"It took me a while to learn that you were an entirely different kettle of fish," he said with a faint smile.

"You say the most romantic things."

"A slippery fish, though. You nearly got away." He put his arms around her and pulled her back into the couch cushions until they were lying side by side. He gave a deep sigh of release that let out all the tension in his body.

She relaxed as well. Again he was teasing, ironic, seductive.

"An angelfish," he murmured, nibbling on her earlobe.

She slipped her arms around his neck and pressed against his long, hard body. Yes, this was the Nick she knew.

"Definitely not a cold fish." There was a pause while he made double sure of that. "So, what am I?" he asked when he raised his head. He took them back to their first night together as if he could erase all the strain and unhappiness that had come between them since then.

"Nick, this is such a silly game," she said, but she was laughing.

"You're just stalling for time, trying to come up with something really horrible."

"No, I'm not." She thought as well as she could think, given that his hands were roving over the curves of her body with distracting skill. "All right, you're a bullhead."

"I knew it. A common, yellow-bellied fish favored by Iowan anglers. And you thought I said such romantic things."

"A bullhead is a relative of the catfish." She, too, was willing to evoke the spell of that night.

His arms tightened around her, hugging her to him with a sudden fierceness, before he released her and stood up to get rid of his clothes. Feverishly he pulled his sweater over his head. Jeans fell in quick succession to the floor. He straightened up and caught her watching him.

He was beautiful to behold in his nakedness with his strong, lean torso and powerful thighs. With his legs planted firmly apart like a giant astride the world, he held out his hands to her. "Fishy, fishy in the brook, come and bite upon my hook," he recited, his lips quirked into an impish smile.

"I was right," she said, eyebrows raised in mock disdain. "You are common." Nevertheless, she rose and went over to him, shedding clothes as she went.

They slowly made their way into the bedroom and onto the bed, limbs too entangled for speedy progress. Their hands and tongues explored each other's bodies, feeling, tasting, hungry for love. Susan didn't think she would ever tire of the touching but before she knew it, touching wasn't enough. She pulled him into her, her hands unceasingly moving along the smooth lines of his back and buttocks. Their joining delivered a full voltage shock, paralyzing them with sensation.

Susan moved first, her body quivering beneath him. He opened his eyes and, to his utter astonishment, saw that she was shaking with laughter. "What the . . . ?"

"Nick," she gasped, clutching his shoulders. "I just thought of another fish. At least, I think it's a fish."

"Your timing is a little off here, Susan," he muttered under his breath.

"No, no, you'll like it. I promise."

"All right," he said reluctantly. "What is it?"

"An electric eel!"

As promised, a big grin spread across his face. "You are the damnedest woman I've ever met." He bent his head to kiss her. The kiss was a laughing, playful kiss that half missed her smiling lips, but even this glancing touch was enough to abruptly sober them. Games were forgotten, laughter was forgotten, even words were forgotten as they made love, their bodies speaking a magical language of their own.

Afterward, Susan nestled in Nick's arms. His heart beat steadily beneath her cheek, as soothing as waves on the beach. "There's one other thing I don't understand about *Fumbling the Ball*," she said lazily. "I knew that Rick was supposed to be you because I recognized Pamela Whitbread's description of your body. She was certainly letter-perfect on that."

"Jealous?"

She did not deign to answer. "However, I would have never recognized you in the character. I mean, Rick was stupid and illiterate, an insensitive, sexually boorish clod."

"You did say that I was common."

"Did I? What on earth made me say that, I wonder," she teased. "I must have been mad, quite mad. You are uncommon."

"Go on, tell me more."

"Why should I feed your male vanity?"

"Because so far you've nearly starved it to death.... Was that a harrumph I just heard? Or merely a guffaw?"

She felt the hurt that lay buried beneath his banter. Raising herself on her elbow, she looked him straight in the eyes. "You are a wonderful lover. When we make love, I lose all sense of who I am. Teachers have a terrible habit of listening to their students express their opinions and then responding, 'Yes, but,' There's always a qualification, a limitation, a negative following the positive. After years of repetition, we start to live our lives that way. 'Yes, but,' When I'm making love with you, it's only yes."

He hugged her close to his chest, quelling the little voice in him that said, *Yes, but you still haven't said you love me.*

When she had settled back down in the crook of his arm, he answered her question. "I may have been twenty-six-years-old when I met Pamela, but I was about as sexually experienced as an adolescent. In high school, I was too caught up in sports to spend much time chasing girls. College was more of the same except that sports took up less time and studies took up more. Of course, I wasn't celibate," he hastened to add.

"Of course not," Susan agreed, smothering a smile. What man ever was?

"There were always girls who were willing to have sex with me."

"Women," she automatically corrected.

"No," he said seriously, surprising her. "They were girls, girls who desperately wanted to be seen with the captain of the football team, girls who had too much to drink at parties, girls who traded sex for love with boys who traded love for sex. I was no saint. If they offered, I took them up on it without much thought or care. When my father died, even that stopped, part of my penance, I suppose.

"Pamela was the first adult woman I had ever been with and she expected more than backseat fumblings. She wanted conversation for one thing and I didn't have anything to say. I hadn't been anywhere or read anything except accounting books for six years. I hadn't been to a movie, a concert, a play, a parade. I had no finesse." Strangely, wonderfully, it didn't bother him to talk about it now. "One of the reasons Pamela's little exposé hurt so much was that even I could see the truth in it. I vowed that no one would ever be able to accuse me of such ignorance and ineptitude again. I sold the business and went to Europe to do The Grand Tour. I stayed for five years, making up for deficiencies in my education." He smiled as he remembered the string of beautiful, sophisticated women who had been only too happy to contribute to his education.

"I learned to play and when I came back home, I was determined not to fall into the steady grind of business again. I had enough money to live comfortably for the rest of my life, but I knew idleness would get me into just as much trouble as too much work had done. In Venice, I had met an architect who was committed to restoring the beautiful old buildings that were crumbling into the ground from centuries of neglect. He was a fascinating fanatic on the subject and for six months, I was his willing pupil. I learned so much from him—art, sculpture, history, architecture. You would like him, I think. Perhaps we could go there this summer."

This summer. It seemed so far away. Susan discovered that she had stopped thinking of the future. It was too fragile and unpredictable to consider. Six months ago, she would have never believed that she would be married by New Year's. Who knew what the next six months would bring?

"When I came back from Europe, I saw that we were no different than the Venetians. The beautiful Victorian houses I used to drive by on my way to work had been replaced by ugly apartment complexes. I decided to do my bit to stop the destruction. That's how I got into restoration work.

"Still, it wasn't enough. I needed something stimulating for my mind. So Jack Philby and I founded Roughwood Press and I started to volunteer at The Literacy Center. I built up a good life, balancing body and mind, work and play. I thought I had taken care of everything until I met you."

"Me? What do I have to do with it?"

"You made me realize I had forgotten to take care of my heart."

"Very nicely put," she said, patting his cheek, trying to keep it light, although her pulse was pounding once again.

"Would you prefer something more inarticulate? 'Hey, babee, babee, ah luv ya.'"

She smiled at that, relieved at his change in tone.

He plopped a kiss down on top of her head, rolled over and swung his legs over the edge of the bed. "I'm hungry," he announced. He stood up and stretched his arms above his head, every muscle lean and defined.

Susan felt a familiar stirring and averted her eyes.

He held out his hand. "Let's make dinner."

She put her hand in his and allowed him to haul her out of bed into his arms. He held her for a minute, singing an old popular love song against her cheek as he danced with her in place, swaying back and forth.

"I'm happy," he said simply. "Thank you."

She pulled back slightly.

"I know, I know," he continued, "you don't want me to be happy. You're afraid of happiness."

She was startled, taken unawares by his perception. She had never thought about it before, but it was true that if someone asked, "How are you?" she would never go farther than a conservative "Okay."

"You're a typical Minnesotan with deep abiding pessimism bred by midwestern weather. The revenge theory of weather—if it's nice today, we'll pay for it tomorrow." He pulled a robe out of the closet and put it on, tying the cloth belt around his waist. "The human version is that if I'm happy today, I'll be sad tomorrow. Moreover, the happier I am now, the more miserable I'll be later. So you guard against happiness in an emotional protection racket. You'll freeze in that," he said when he saw her reaching for her flimsy negligee. "And I won't be able to concentrate on my dinner. One appetite at a time." He handed her another warm robe, which came down to her ankles.

"I'll make a deal with you," he continued. "I'm a gambling man. Just let me be happy. I'll take the risk and you have nothing to lose. In fact, you'll be safer than ever because I'll be a lightning rod at your side, absorbing all the happiness and misery in the immediate vicinity."

"Be happy then." She was going to leave it at that. She wished she could blithely accept his love and return it with her own, regardless of the consequences. She wanted to be free and giddy and passionate. She wanted to be impulsive where she was hesitant, trusting where she was skeptical, but something in her held back. The rigorous discipline in which she had been schooled was not so easily discarded, the bereavement and anxiety of the past few years not so easily overcome, the independence not so easily compromised.

"I don't want you to get hurt, that's all," she said as she followed him into the kitchen.

He found the florist's box behind the empty brown grocery bags, shoved way back against the canisters lining the counter. "I forgot, I bought these for you," he said, turning toward her.

"Oh, Nick," she said, a guilty expression on her face. She opened the box and lifted out the roses. Transported from cold to heat, deprived of water for hours, their heads drooped limply to the side.

"Woman," he said, shaking his head, a twisted smile on his lips, "you're death on roses."

9

THEY SPENT THREE DAYS at Nick's cabin, hiking in the woods, cooking elaborate meals together, making love and lounging in front of the fire. If they could have lived there forever in splendid isolation, Susan knew that she could have easily loved Nick with the same uncomplicated passion that he lavished upon her, but all too soon the honeymoon was drawing to a close and she could feel the muscles in her face tightening with renewed tension.

On the night before they were to return to Minneapolis, Susan looked up from her book and said, "Where are we going to live?"

"Where do you want to live?" Nick countered.

"I'd like to live in my house." She prepared herself for debate. Compared to his beautiful nineteenth-century carriage house, her home looked like the old two-story farmhouse farmers hauled away and converted into a rat-ridden grain bin before building the ranch-style house of their dreams. Nevertheless, she had worked too hard to buy it on her own to relinquish it so soon.

"Fine," he said. "Then it's settled." He started to read where he had left off.

Susan looked at him uncertainly. Had it been that easy?

Nick felt her eyes upon him and looked up. "I take it that I will be living there, too?"

"Of course," she answered, nonplussed.

"Good." He picked up his book again.

They read for another half hour or, at least, Nick did. All Susan could think about were the domestic details that were about to come crashing down on her head. What would he do with his house? His furniture? What about money? Would they share expenses? If so, how would they split the cost? Straight fifty-fifty or a proportion of their incomes? How would they allocate household chores? Oh, no, did he expect her to iron his shirts? Whose idea was this marriage business anyway? His. He did expect her to iron his shirts! Would she still be able to study at home? Her tenure decision was coming up soon. Would she get it? How had her marriage affected the decision?

"I start school in four days," she volunteered into the silence.

"That soon?"

"Yes."

Twenty minutes passed, the only sound in the room the flaming wood snapping sparks in the fireplace. Nick turned the pages of his book at regular intervals but Susan's lay open on her lap, the pages fanning in one direction, then the other.

"What time do you want to leave for the city tomorrow?" she asked.

"Good book?" he asked dryly, marking his place with his finger.

"What?"

"Is that a good book you're reading?"

She frowned. "Not particularly. Why?" Her face cleared. "Sorry, am I bothering you? I didn't mean to interrupt. I hate it when people are constantly interrupting when you're trying to read. Or when they read all the best bits in the Sunday paper out loud to you before you can read them yourself."

"Despicable," he agreed. "I thought we'd leave in the morning after breakfast. All right?"

She nodded and picked up her book but within minutes, it had fallen to her lap again. Finally she gave up. "I'm going for a walk."

Nick waited for an invitation to accompany her.

"I won't be long." Her voice was muffled as she pulled another sweater over her head. With the bright red parka on top of that, she was padded so thickly she could barely bend over to lace up her heavy hiking boots. She put on insulated mittens and waved at him as she clumped to the door.

"You look like the Michelin tire man," he commented from the couch.

Her mittens were so stiff that she couldn't grasp the doorknob. "Now I remember what it was like to be five years old in the winter," she grumbled as she pulled off a mitten.

"Do you want some help?"

"I can do it." She opened the door and stepped out into the cold. The frigid air bit at her fingers as she struggled to put her right hand back into the mitten. She wrapped a scarf around her nose and mouth to warm the night air before it penetrated to her lungs. By the time she had walked the length of the narrow driveway leading from the cabin to the main road, the ice had already crystallized from her moist breath into the porous weave of the wool scarf.

She followed the snow-packed tire tracks on the road, so preoccupied that she was oblivious to the night sounds coming from the woods. Too many questions, too many uncertainties. What would their life be like when they went back to the Cities? Would Nick accept her friendship with Richard? Did he want to have children? Did she? How many? How soon? With a shock, she realized that she had used her hectic schedule as an excuse not to deal with these questions before. Deep inside, she knew that if she had confronted these issues earlier, she might never have gone through with the wedding. And now she was going to pay for it.

She broke into a run. When the stitch in her side grew too painful, she slowed down until she had caught her breath enough to run again. she could feel the sweat trickle down between her breasts. Still she ran on.

Nick read peacefully for a while after Susan left for her walk but gradually he started glancing up at the clock, noting the passing time with increasing frequency. She said she wouldn't be gone long. How long had she meant?

Time, which had always seemed to him entirely reliable, now seemed as capricious as the northern lights. The three days he and Susan had spent here had passed by so quickly they were like witnessing brilliant lightning, the actual flash over in a second, the afterimage forever etched on the retina. The minutes she had been gone, on the other hand, stretched out as endless and empty as a black hole in space.

Should he go after her? It was clear that she had not wanted him to come with her. He tried not to dwell on that. But what if she was hurt? The temperature had dropped steadily since they had arrived. This morning, the snow had crunched underfoot when they had taken a walk and all day long they had seen sun dogs hovering in the chilly sky, a harbinger of even colder weather to come. She would not survive long out there tonight.

He peered out the window into the dark night, searching for a moving shadow. There! At last! By the time Susan stomped her feet on the front steps, he was once again lounging on the couch, absorbed in his reading. "Back already?" he asked when she came in. "Have a good walk?"

She sat down heavily on a chair near the door, too tired to move. "It's very cold out tonight," she managed to say. After a minute's rest, she pulled off her mittens, untied the hood of her parka and pushed it back.

He could see that her hair was damp, the matted curls clinging wetly to her forehead.

"I think I'll take a hot bath and turn in." She slowly took off the rest of her wraps and made her way into the bathroom.

Soon Nick could hear the sound of water running into the deep bathtub and then splashing as Susan stepped into the hot, scented water. He visualized her sinking up to her neck in the water, her head resting against the sloping white enamel. If he were to join her, he could cup the small round soap in his palm and run his hand all over her body, soaping and gently stroking with the tips of his fingers at the same time. He shook his head and tried to read, but his mind kept returning to Susan.

Why was he waiting for an invitation? he thought crossly. She was his wife and he knew that she would respond, even against her will, to his touch. But he didn't want to persuade or seduce. He wanted her to come to him as fiercely and imperiously as she had done their first night together.

When she opened the bathroom door, a cloud of steam billowed out into the room. Through the mist, he could see that her head was wrapped in a turban and that she wore one of his heavy robes. She came over and sat cross-legged in front of the fire to towel her hair dry. He watched her lean toward the flame, rubbing her head with the thick fluffy towel, running her fingers through the curls to shake out the droplets of water.

As soon as her hair was dry, she got up to go to bed. She hesitated by the couch, then put her hand on his shoulder. "Good night," she said.

He covered her hand with his own. "Good night." His dark eyes searched her face for any sign of what was troubling her, but she gave nothing away.

Nick stayed up for a couple of hours after she had gone to bed, staring into the fire. He had been so sure that she would grow to love him. Sometimes he thought she already did but for the first time, he began to wonder whether their marriage could ever be what he wanted it to be.

When he went into the bedroom, Susan was asleep. He got undressed and slipped into bed beside her, taking care not to wake her. She slept on her stomach, head turned to the side, right knee thrust out for balance. Her newly washed hair was a soft tangle of curls that tempted him to bury his face in their fresh fragrance.

He studied her face. She was not classically beautiful nor was she pretty in the traditional cute and pert style favored by 1950's movies and *Playboy* magazine. Neither was she like those wild children who look angelic and thus redeem themselves when they sleep. Her beauty showed itself when she was awake, particularly when she was matching wits with him. That was when she was most alive; that was when she was as entrancing to watch as fireworks on the Fourth of July. Eyes sparkling with excitement, hands gesturing with grace and force, she let go of her natural restraint and came into her own. She let go in bed, too, not initially, not willingly; she fought against relinquishing control but once she conceded the fight, she was beautiful.

Asleep, she was drained of life and almost plain, vulnerable. He gritted his teeth to choke back the protectiveness that welled up in him. Gently he pulled her toward him until her extended leg rested upon his thighs and her head was pillowed in the hollow of his shoulder. With one arm around her back, cradling her to him, and the other resting on her head as if in benediction, he, too, fell asleep.

BY LATE AFTERNOON the next day, they were back in Minneapolis. The city streets were lined with mounds of snow, which was dirty in contrast to the pristine whiteness up north. Christmas lights still blinked in store windows, illuminating the Happy New Year signs.

"It's New Year's Eve tonight," Susan said in surprise as they drove past a noisy bar where revelers were getting an early start.

"Do you want to celebrate? We could eat out, go dancing, or I was invited to several parties, if you're in the mood."

"Do you mind if we stayed in? The thought of a loud crowded party after the peace and quiet of the cabin is a bit daunting."

"That's fine with me. I've never cared for New Year's Eve. There's always a tinge of desperation under the goodwill." He pulled into her driveway, shut off the ignition and turned toward her. "We're home."

Home. Susan shivered although the car was warm enough. She opened her door, got out and took a deep breath. Even the air was different in the city. It was heavier somehow; it weighed one down. She and Nick each grabbed a suitcase and hiked through the unshoveled snow on her sidewalk to the back door.

"I know it's traditional for the groom to carry the bride over the threshold," he said while she dug for her keys in her purse, "but I don't think tradition takes into account either Minnesota winters or the modern woman. One pictures the groom sleek in a tuxedo, Robert Young or Fred Astaire, the bride lithe in a white gown.... Hmmmm, no one comes to mind but you."

She glanced up at him and smiled before continuing to dig for her keys.

"One does not picture the happy couple padded in six inches of goose down, as roly poly as the Campbell's Soup kids. In the traditional ritual, the groom picks up the bride and sweeps her gracefully through the door of their first home, a home they have chosen together, a home full of French doors, bright sunlight, and pink geraniums."

Anyone who didn't know Nick would think he was talking nonsense to mask his nervousness, she thought as she sorted through the shredded tissues, paper clips and rubber bands, loose change, old grocery shopping lists and emergency sewing kit in her purse.

"I am more likely to stumble over the threshold with you in my arms. You will accidentally kick the wall with your wet hiking boots and leave a mysterious footprint four feet off the floor. We will be written up in the *World Weekly News*. We will charge admission. 'You've seen the Shroud of Turin. You've seen Lucy from the Olduvai. Now see the amazing, the incredible, the fantastic, the Mysterious Mark of Red Wing.'"

Trust Nick, it was entertaining nonsense. Her fingers closed over the round key ring at the bottom of her purse. "Found it!" She unlocked the door and pushed it open. She had started to pick up her suitcase when Nick caught her by the wrist. She looked at him and read the half-embarrassed expression on his face. "But you want to do it anyway," she guessed with amusement.

He nodded and held out his arms.

She put her suitcase down and let him scoop her up. He carried her lightly in his arms for all of their bulky clothing and stepped through the narrow back door with nary a bump, scrape, stumble or mysterious footprint.

"You did that very well," she complimented.

"I've had lots of practice."

"Do tell."

"I've been angling armfuls of lumber through doorways for two years."

"And one piece of deadwood is much like any other?"

He smiled and kissed her, a slow, warm, welcome-home kiss, claiming her mouth with his lips and tongue. She clasped her arms around his neck and parted her lips to receive him. After a breathless interval, he pulled away. "I'll get the rest of the suitcases."

She watched him go, her senses disordered and confused. It felt so strange to be here in her house with him. He was moving in...forever. The thought was good and scary all at the same time.

By the time he had all the luggage carried in and taken upstairs to the bedroom, she had made tea. They sat down at the card table in the kitchen and found themselves without one word to say. The silence grew uncomfortable, portentous.

"It's kind of like 'This is the first day of the rest of your life,' isn't it?" she finally observed.

"I'm glad you're making such long-range plans for us," he replied, wanting to ignore the panic underlying her words. But after a moment, he asked, "Are you trying to tell me that the honeymoon is over?"

"Well, here we are." She gestured around her and the gesture encompassed her empty house, Humboldt College four blocks away, Minneapolis and the whole real world. "I have to get back to work. I'm not prepared for spring term." She could feel him withdraw as she spoke. Damn Pamela Whitbread, she thought explosively, and damn Nicholas Taurage for making me feel guilty.

He swallowed the last of his tea. "Then I suppose I had better get back to work, too." The table rocked gently against his knees when he put the cup down on its stained cardboard surface. "We need to do something about this house."

"I was going to work on it when I had more time and money." She was as defensive as a mother with a child lagging behind in the developmental charts.

"And when would that be?"

"The twelfth of never," she retorted. He knew perfectly well that she would never be able to properly fix up the place on her own.

"I'll work on it," he volunteered. "Has it ever been rewired? Or do you know?"

"Yes, I know!"

"Sorry."

"It has not been rewired."

"What about insulation?" He got up to wander around the room, his expert eye scanning for problems and solutions. "Has it been reinsulated?"

"Not that, either."

"Plumbing?"

"Yes, I do have plumbing," she replied acidly, but he had his head buried underneath the kitchen sink peering at the pipes and didn't appear to have heard her.

"I wish I had my tools here," he said when he crawled out. "Do you have a tape measure?"

She silently fetched a tape measure from the kitchen drawer.

"Great. How about a screwdriver and a pair of pliers?"

The drawer once again produced the requisite tools.

"Now we just need paper and pencil and we'll get down to work." As always, starting a new house project absorbed him, cheered him. Everything he gazed upon was full of possibilities. And this house was especially important, especially full of possibilities. "It will be a good working together," he continued.

That was a matter of opinion, Susan decided crossly some time later. Nick's version of working together involved him measuring, poking and prying in every room of the house while she trailed behind him taking notes. For five hours. The charming man she had married, the devastating lover, the decent human being, vanished. In his place roamed an architectural Mr. Hyde.

"Nick, it's nearly midnight," she protested to the square black hole in the ceiling.

His head peeked over the edge of the attic floor. He had bits of fluffy insulation stuck in his hair and dust streaked across his cheek. One look at the expression on her face convinced him that perhaps they had worked long enough for one evening. His head disappeared and was immediately replaced by his long legs, which dangled over the edge for a second as he positioned himself to jump. He descended in a cloud of cobwebs, splinters and fiberglass.

She sneezed.

"Bless you," he said, patting her on the back. "I saved a bottle of champagne for the occasion. It's in the refrigerator. Just let me clean up a bit first."

She waited for him in the kitchen, sitting at the card table, unhappily studying an electrical outlet that Nick had dismantled in his examination of her apparently substandard, antiquated, and possibly hazardous wiring. They had been back less than twelve hours and already he was turning her life upside down. Something had to be done. She was going to have to take a stand.

Within ten minutes, he was back. He pulled the champagne out of the refrigerator with a flourish, uncorked the bottle with a satisfying pop and poured the cool sparkling wine into two tulip glasses. Eyeing the card table and folding chairs with disfavor, he said, "Isn't there anywhere else we can sit?"

"Not really."

They ended up lounging on the ugly mustard carpet in front of the drafty fireplace that was too sooty to use. "It's like being married to Grandma Moses," Nick complained. He was sitting uncomfortably with his back against the wall, his legs sprawled out in front of him.

Susan lay on her back with her knees raised and crossed, one foot bouncing up and down in the air. She balanced her champagne glass on her stomach. "Just think of the advantages," she said, turning her head toward him. "No whatnots to dust."

"No bric-a-brac."

"No knickknacks."

"No objet d'art. Only this awful carpet. This is going to be one of the first things to go," he declared unilaterally.

That did it. "What?" She rolled over on her side and set the glass down on the floor. "I love this carpet."

"You're not serious."

"Yes, I am."

How could she possibly like it? Had he misjudged her intelligence? Was she educable? "There is probably a beautiful hardwood floor underneath and I have an old Oriental rug that would perfectly fit the room."

"No, I want the carpet as is."

"Susan, I get jaundiced just looking at the thing. It offends every aesthetic sensibility."

"I don't care."

He took a deep breath and considered whether he could live with mustard nylon pile. "You really want to keep it?"

"I really do."

"It's a matter of principles," he said pleadingly.

"Love me, love my carpet." She was adamant. They could hear the Humboldt College campanile begin to ring in the New Year in the distance. "Make up your mind."

"The carpet stays," he said reluctantly. If they filled up the room with a lot of furniture, like wall-to-wall furniture, maybe it wouldn't be so bad. Maybe.

She sat up and clinked her glass with his. "Happy New Year." She bent over to kiss him to hide her relief. If they could compromise over their differences, their mutual commitment to work, maybe it wouldn't be so bad. Maybe.

"Happy New Year," he grumbled back.

She let him suffer for a minute and then said, "I have a present for you."

"Something good I hope," he answered, sliding his hand along her thigh.

"Not that," she exclaimed as she laughingly slapped his hand away.

His hand continued up her thigh. She could see that he was not going to be easy to distract and she could feel her own attention span slipping rather badly. "I'm giving you the carpet," she blurted out.

That stopped him. "What? But you just said...
Whatever happened to 'I love this carpet'? 'I can't live
without this carpet'? 'This carpet is life's breath to me'?
'Bone of my bone, flesh of my flesh'?"

"I lied."

"You, you minx! You viper, you vixen." He made a
move to administer swift and certain punishment, but
she had anticipated his reaction and rolled away. She was
scrambling to her feet when he caught her by the ankles
and brought her down again. Both champagne glasses
went flying, spilling their contents on the carpet.

"Look what you've done," he panted as he sat astride
her. Susan was flat on her back with her arms pinned
above her head. "You Gila monster, you newt." He was
ad-libbing now.

"Mercy, sir, please, have mercy." Her begging would
have been more believable if she hadn't been giggling.

He leaned over and kissed her hard on the lips. Her
tongue did battle with his in a delicious war that sent
reason in retreat.

"Mercy," she breathed in quite a different intonation.

"I think it's time for bed," he said. However, he was too
busy trailing kisses from her temple to the soft hollow at
the base of her neck to get up.

Her eyes closed, she nodded her incoherent consent
but made no move to go upstairs. In fact, when he released her wrists so he could use his hands as well as
mouth and tongue to touch her, she twined her arms
around his neck and drew him closer. "We'd be more
comfortable in bed," she murmured sometime later
without stirring from his arms.

"Mmmmmm," he agreed as he unbuttoned her blouse,
unfastened her bra and licked the stiff peaks of her
breasts.

She dug her fingers into his hair, holding his head, willing him to continue. When the liquid sensation pooled in her abdomen and lifted her hips off the floor as if she were floating on a deep blue sea, she pushed him away, unsnapped her jeans, and slipped out of them.

"The bed would be softer," Nick said as he pulled his sweater over his head and unbuttoned the top buttons on his shirt while Susan worked her way up from the bottom. She nuzzled his firm stomach as she went, the dark hair on his torso tickling her face, the feel of his body a warm caress against her cheek in contrast to the cool room air. Eager to be naked and free, he pulled off his jeans in one quick movement.

"So, do you want to go upstairs?" Susan asked in a distracted voice as she stroked his tensed muscular thighs, her fingertips moving upward until she reached his hardness. With the tip of her tongue, she outlined the contours of his manhood.

"Too late," he gasped. He tried unsuccessfully to slow down the urgency that raced through his body. Groaning, he laid back on the champagne drenched carpet carrying her with him.

The sight of Nick's lean muscles rippling over his rib cage and the tendons in his neck stretched taut under the skin as he curled downward excited Susan as much as his touch. He was all flesh and blood, bone and sinew, powerful and delicate at the same time. With every feeling concentrated in his loins, he was unaware of the tears that fell on his face as she cried at his beauty and at the sharp joy of their lovemaking.

Afterward, they lay together for only a few minutes before both of them were shivering. "I'm freezing," Nick said, sitting up. He twisted an arm around and felt his back. "I'm also wet."

Susan rose on one elbow, leaned over and licked him. "You taste like champagne."

"A champagne icicle." He stood up, holding out his hand to help her up as well. "Let's have a shower and go to bed."

"Will we actually make it to the bed this time?" she said as they embraced under the hot pulsating spray of water.

"If at first you don't succeed, try, try again."

Sometime later, Nick was nearly asleep, warm and pleasantly exhausted, when he heard Susan whisper, "Nick? Are you awake?"

"No," he mumbled, although he ruffled her curls in response before drifting back into a half-asleep, half-awake state.

"Nick," she whispered more insistently.

The seriousness of her voice penetrated his consciousness. "What?" He forced his eyes open.

"I want this to work. Us, I mean." She was curled up on her side, facing him, with one arm tucked under her head as a pillow. She reached out and rested her other hand against his cheek.

"So do I," he said softly.

"But tonight you just took over. This used to be my house, then all of a sudden it became yours, and I didn't have anything to say about it anymore."

"I'm sorry. I promise to tread more lightly."

"But I don't want you tiptoeing around as if I were highly explosive nitroglycerin, either."

He expelled his breath in a sigh of frustration. "Susan, I'm damned if I do and damned if I don't."

She bit her lower lip. "I know it sounds that way. I don't mean to be unfair."

He could see her confusion. "Oh, hell," he said, shrugging and pulling her into his arms. "Life is unfair. Don't worry about it, Susie Q."

She raised her head from his shoulder. "My family used to call me that when I was little."

"Did they ever tell you what the Q stands for?"

She shook her head. "I didn't think it meant anything in particular. It was just a nickname."

"Well, in your case," he said wryly, "it stands for quibble, quaver and qualify. Now go to sleep."

10

Two days later Susan went back to school and Nick tore out the bathtub.

"Couldn't we wait to do some of this?" she asked him from the hall just before she left. She was dressed in a navy wool suit and navy heels and didn't dare step foot into the upstairs bathroom because a fine white film of crumbling plaster covered the floor.

Nick was crouched in the tiny tub, pounding on the faucets, trying to break the rusty grip that had frozen them to the water pipes twenty years ago. His biceps bulged with effort as he tightened the wrench and pulled until the faucets gave way with a grating noise that made the hair stand up on Susan's scalp.

"Why are you tearing out the tub? It works."

"When I got in to take a bath last night," he replied over his shoulder, "my knees were level with my chin. It's just too small."

She watched helplessly as he picked up the crowbar and pried more plaster away from the plumbing so he could see what he was doing.

"Aren't you going into school?" he asked, looking up from his work.

"Yes, I was just leaving." She paused. "Actually I was hoping to brush my teeth," she said, pointing in the direction of the bathroom sink, which was still in one piece.

"I turned off the water, sorry." He got up, brushed his hands clean on his jeans and came over to kiss her goodbye. "I love you. Have a good day."

"Have a good day," she echoed unconvincingly against his lips and retreated to Humboldt.

She was brushing her teeth in the third floor Grantley Hall bathroom when Molly walked in.

"Well, if it isn't the blushing bride, or the brushing bride as the case may be. How's married life?"

"It has its moments," she said with a slow smile, "and then it has its moments," she concluded, rolling her eyes in exasperation.

"That about sums it up," Molly agreed. "And which moment are we on today?"

"The latter. Nick is single-handedly demolishing my house. He's a fiend."

"You're lucky that he's handy. Miguel and I are both hopeless when it comes to home repairs. If I so much as change a light bulb, I have to recite 'righty, tighty, lefty, loosey' to remember which way to turn. Humiliating, isn't it?" She dropped the subject and hopped on to the next. "Are you free for lunch today? Why don't you come with me to the Faculty Club?"

"I don't know," Susan shook her head dubiously.

"You haven't been back there for ages and it's time. FTP is going to start meeting soon."

"Once more into the fray?"

"This is the last round, kiddo. Come out fighting."

So, with fists sheathed in velvet gloves, Susan went back to the Faculty Club flanked by Molly and Richard. To her delight, she discovered that, unlike the December faculty meeting when she had been pariah of the month, she was now sought after.

"May we join you?" Roger Perkins, Phillip Hunter and Ken Bjorklund stood by the table, food trays in hand.

Susan and Molly exchanged covert significant glances.

"Certainly," Susan said, sliding her chair closer to Richard to make room for six people at a table meant for four.

The three newcomers unloaded their trays, pulled up additional chairs and squeezed in. Initially talk focused on the beginning of term with everyone comparing student enrollments in their classes and complaining about departmental budgets for photocopying, film rentals and library orders.

Susan felt as though she had been granted a reprieve. It was as if the past three disastrous months had never happened. She had been given another chance, free and clear.

But then the conversation turned.

"What is Nick up to these days?" Roger Perkins asked.

"I saw him at the hardware store yesterday," Phillip Hunter chimed in.

"He's working on the house," Susan said with a stiff smile.

"Must be nice to have a handyman in the family."

"Yes."

Ken Bjorklund took up the torch. "A bunch of the Humboldt faculty get together once a month to play poker. Do you think Nick would be interested in joining us?"

"All men," Molly muttered on one side of her. "Women have never been invited."

"Is Nick going to be at the faculty potluck next week?" Ken asked. "We could talk to him about it then."

"If he is going to be there, I'll bring the article on Roughwood Press that I clipped from the *St. Paul Pio-*

neer Press for him," Roger added. "Did he see it? It was in just before Christmas. Nice article."

"Too bad Nick isn't up for tenure," Richard muttered on the other side of her. "He'd be a shoo-in."

Susan pushed her plate aside. Somewhere along the line, she had lost her appetite.

A MONTH LATER, Nick stood back and surveyed the finished bathroom. It was the best work he had ever done. He had achieved a balance between simplicity and luxury, between modern convenience and antique charm. Like an artist, his eye picked up the bits of color that drew one irresistibly into the room. The gleaming enamel of the new bathtub built for two. The jewel tones of the stained-glass window. The softer shades in the plush towels. The dark warmth of the oak trim. It was inspired; it was meaningless.

He went downstairs and poured himself a cup of coffee from the thermos. Sipping from a thick white mug, he wandered into the living room. The first week back from the honeymoon, he had called a chimney sweep to clean the fireplace. The ugly mustard carpet was gone. He had ripped it up and, as he had predicted, solid hardwood floors lay underneath. He sank into the comfortable old leather couch he had brought over from his house before he sold it.

He had accomplished a lot of work in the past month, but it was not enough. He was failing in more important ways. He had discovered that working on a house, no matter how run-down the house or how ambitious the remodeling plans, was child's play compared to negotiating the intricacies of marriage.

He knew Susan was worried about tenure. She came back from school each day a little more preoccupied and distant. In his heart, he raged against Humboldt for putting her through this ordeal and, God help him, he was beginning to rage against Susan for letting them.

He did everything he could to make it easy for her. He quit working on the house as soon as she came home and spent the evenings reading Roughwood Press manuscripts while she graded papers or prepared lectures. This quiet life would have suited him if, once in a while, she would have looked up from her papers and smiled at him. If, once in a while, she would have come over and sat in his lap, put her arms around his neck, pulled his head down, and kissed him with tenderness as well as passion.

It wasn't as if she wasn't trying. He moved through every room of the house like a devouring locust and she never complained about the mess. She admired every finished project. She carefully slotted free time for them on the weekends so they could go visit her mother or his. It was all so damn correct that it was driving him crazy!

He could hear Susan's footsteps on the front porch. Abruptly he set the coffee mug down on the floor and went to meet her.

"Hello," she started to say but he cut her off with a hard, almost angry kiss. She tried to pull away, dropping her briefcase to the floor and pushing on his chest with her hands. He held her more tightly, bending her head back with the force of his kiss. "What are you doing?" she panted when she succeeded in breaking free.

"I want you," he said roughly, unbuttoning her coat and shoving it back off her shoulders.

"I just got home," she protested.

"I don't want to hear any excuses." He knew he was behaving like a brute but couldn't help himself. He would try anything to get a reaction from her, anything to break down the barriers going up between them.

"Stop it, Nick!"

The look of angry fear on her face penetrated his madness and he stopped cold. "Sorry," he muttered half in shock at the violence he had nearly wreaked on her and on their relationship. He backed off and headed for the basement where he tried to concentrate on the bookcase he was building. Although the basement was icy cold, his face was flushed hot with shame. No wonder she held back from him. Not since Pamela Whitbread had he acted so stupidly.

He worked doggedly for hours until his fingers were too cramped to hold a piece of sandpaper. Then he showered and went upstairs. Susan was already in bed with the light out. She was turned on her side away from him as he came into the bedroom. He moved silently so as not to wake her and lay down on the edge of the bed, giving her as much room as possible.

He felt her turn over and face him. "Nick?"

He opened his eyes. Her face was faintly lit in the moonlight coming through the lace curtain at the bedroom window. She looked beautiful and he wanted her so badly that he didn't dare make a move. In one careless moment, he had betrayed the tenuous trust so painstakingly established between them. "Sorry," he whispered once again.

"Everyone makes mistakes, Nick," she replied softly and stroked his cheek with her hand. She invited him into her arms, into her warmth, and he accepted the invitation with passion made more intense with gratitude.

They might not have laughter and nonsense anymore, Nick thought fiercely before he entered her, but at least they had this. They still had this!

LOCKED AWAY in her windowless office on a Friday afternoon in March, Susan was unaware that the snow that
had been falling slowly all morning had changed to an
icy rain that pelleted the city. By one o'clock, the local
radio station started announcing school closings and by
two, the list of not only closed schools and businesses but
canceled social events was so long that it completely
preempted all other programming.

No born Minnesotan was truly surprised. The boys'
state basketball tournament was being held in town and
it was a long-standing tradition that weather of disastrous proportions always occurred during the tournament. Basketball fans, particularly the high-school kids,
almost counted on it and were strangely disappointed if
the year was mild and trouble free. The heroism of their
team's efforts deserved truly epic storms. Bad weather
was appropriate.

Susan read on, far removed from the traffic backed up
on the freeway as everyone tried to get home before conditions deteriorated any further. Forewarned by annual
spring precedent, most people were already safe at home
by five o'clock when the highway department announced that the roads were so slippery that even their
massive sanding trucks couldn't get enough traction to
make it up the slight rise of the entrance ramps. The city
didn't screech to a halt so much as slip and slide to a halt.

The uninterrupted silence in Grantley was so rare and
unexpected a gift that Susan didn't stop to question the
cause. She had just received the new *Social Psychology
Quarterly* in the mail and, although she was disappointed that a review of her book wasn't in it yet, she ea-
gerly devoured its contents.

Her work was increasingly essential to her. She tried
to tell herself that her love of the subject drove her on,

hour after hour, but she knew that she was using her work to avoid Nick. She didn't know how to talk to him anymore. She thought often and longingly of their honeymoon at the cabin. Alone, without outside intrusion, they had been free and natural with each other. She had caught a glimpse of what they could share—silliness, passionate sex and emotional intimacy. But here in the city, they had to deal with the real world and they hadn't yet learned how. Sometimes she wondered if they ever would, but then she would push those thoughts to the back of her mind and work even harder.

She was just finishing an article on the effect of mood on memory when the phone rang. "Professor Harkness," she answered distractedly as she read the final sentence.

"Susan, do you know that we're in the middle of an ice storm? Humboldt called off classes several hours ago. When are you coming home?"

The concern in Nick's voice cut through her concentration. "Sorry," she said, shaking her head, trying to shift gears from abstract thought to physical reality. "I've been reading. How bad is it?"

"It's so bad," Nick replied, unable to resist an Ed McMahon, Johnny Carson line like that, "that even the icicles have to use Poli•Grip to stick to the roof."

"All right," she said, a smile on her lips. "I'm heading out the door. Be home in a few minutes."

But as soon as she stepped outside Grantley Hall onto the glassy sidewalk, she realized that her promise to Nick had been overly optimistic. The entire campus was encased in ice. Each delicate branch on the winter-stripped bushes, the black handrailings on the steps in front of Old Main, and the normally rough brown bark of the tree trunks were all slick and shining with a half inch thick layer of ice. She shuffled a few yards, slowly, tentatively, before stopping to mentally measure the length of the sidewalk stretching out in front of her like an endless mirror in a fun house. At this rate, she would make it home around June.

The wind blew hard, cold and wet around her, its sheer force skidding her across the slick ice against her will. This is crazy, she suddenly decided, her cheeks stinging from the sharp sleet, her eyes squinting against the translucent glare. She would just have to stay the night at Grantley.

Cautiously she turned around and headed toward safety and firm footing. About four feet away from the door, her feet went flying out from under her. She managed to brace her fall with her right arm, but she still landed heavily on her hip. The fall knocked the wind right out of her and she gasped for breath for a minute before recovering sufficiently to feel for damages. She seemed to be all right—no broken bones, but she knew that she was going to have bruises the size of saucers by the next day.

Trying to stand up was another challenge. She got up on her hands and knees but first her legs and then her hands would slip on the cold ice until she felt like a newborn colt trying to stand for the first time in its awkward, gangly life. Finally, with a surreptitious look around the deserted campus, she abandoned all shreds of dignity and crawled the rest of the way to Grantley.

The first thing she did was call Nick. "I can't make it," she said, breathing hard from her exertions. "It's just too slippery."

"How slippery is it?" he asked. He wanted to see if she would play. He knew he should stop testing her for signs of her affection and commitment to him, for signs of their essential synchronism, but he couldn't help himself. If she jokes back, he told himself, she loves me. If she doesn't . . .

"It's so slippery," she responded dryly, "that it gives eels a good name."

Nick expelled his pent-up breath.

"I'm going to have to stay at Humboldt tonight and try to make it home in the morning when it melts. *If* it melts by then." She paused while the lights flickered ominously in her office. "Oh-oh." Total darkness descended. "Oh, no!"

"What is it?" Nick asked anxiously, rising from his seat.

"The lights just went out!" Her heart sank at the thought of spending the whole night alone in the dark but she tried to hide her dismay so he wouldn't worry. "Must be ice on the lines."

"Just stay put," he ordered. "I'll call the electric company to tell them about your lights and I'm sure they will send someone right away to fix them." He didn't tell her that the radio had just announced widespread power outages and estimated that downed areas would be without electricity for at least the night and possibly tomorrow as well. "After all, I'm Rudy Kilowatt, remember? I've got pull. Bye."

He also didn't tell her that he had no intention of leaving her stranded all by herself at the office all night. He didn't want her to worry but, ice or no ice, he was going to join her. "Hang on, Susan," he muttered to himself as he dug in the closet for his old battered ice skates, "I'm on my way."

After she hung up the phone, Susan felt her way to her office door to see if there was any better light in the hall. It wasn't much help. She could make out the dusky outlines of scattered chairs, but the effect was spooky rather than comforting. Her watch, glowing eerily in the dark, indicated that it was six-thirty. What was she going to do all evening? She shivered in the chill of the empty corridor and immediately another horrible thought occurred to her. No electricity meant no heat! She went back into her office and closed the door to preserve the precious warmth.

Six-forty. Was it getting noticeably cooler already or was it just her imagination? Just her imagination, she told herself.

Seven o'clock. All she could think of was the Little Match Girl. Such a sad story. And she didn't even have any matches.

Seven-ten. She could just see Nick tenderly placing roses on her grave. He would make such an attractive widower. She focused on his handsome, grief-stricken face. Standing behind him were both of their mothers, hands linked out of sympathy. And behind them was Pamela Whitbread. And an unknown brunette, a devastating redhead, a voluptuous blonde...

Susan shook herself out of her musings and stood up to stretch. Seven-fifteen. It was going to be a very long night.

She paced up and down for a while until she heard something. Stopping dead still in her tracks, she listened intently, like a deer might listen for the sounds of the hunter tracking it down. She heard the noise again. It sounded like someone heavily ascending the stairs. Someone big, weighed down. Susan never ever went to horror movies, but the ads were inescapable. When she asked herself the question—weighed down with what?— the answer was quickly forthcoming, prepackaged in glorious Technicolor. Chainsaws! Red dripping knives! Axes!

The hairs on Susan's arms stood up like raised hackles as the footsteps climbed the last set of stairs and came toward her office. She backed into the corner as far away from the door as possible. Flattened against the wall, she waited for her entire life to flash before her eyes but all she could think about was whether she had locked the door and that damn blonde lurking in wait for Nick at her funeral.

The footsteps stopped directly in front of her office. She visualized a huge hairy hand reaching for the door handle, pressing down. She heard the door softly swinging open—she hadn't locked it—and got ready to scream. Scream bloody murder. She drew a breath deep into her lungs . . .

"Susan?"

"Nick!" Her recognition was instantaneous. His voice penetrated her cold fear like a laser beam, blasting it to bits. She ran across the room and flung her arms around his neck. "Oh, Nick!"

He hugged her back, choked up with emotion. This was the welcome he had been longing for and had almost given up expecting.

"How on earth did you get here?" she demanded joyously, clinging to him in her relief.

He motioned to the skates hanging over his arm, unwilling to break the spell with mundane words.

"My very own Hans Brinker," she said lightly. "I'm so glad to see you."

They stood there locked in each other's arms for a few minutes before she pulled away. After the initial greeting, both of them seemed at a loss for words.

"I brought provisions," Nick finally said. He handed her the flashlight he carried in one hand, slung off his bulky hiker's backpack, knelt down beside it and began to pull out the goodies he had packed.

Susan exclaimed with delight at each item. Wine, cheese, bread, truffles, candles, matches, a double sleeping bag. "This is better than Christmas," she informed him.

Soon the office was illuminated with the warm dancing light of candles lit on the desk, the bookshelves and the floor. Susan and Nick sat cross-legged on the unzipped spread-out sleeping bag, drinking wine out of chipped coffee cups and eating thickly sliced bread and cheese. "This tastes great," she said, relishing every bite. "There's nothing like a little deprivation to make you appreciate the simple things in life."

"Including me?" he asked.

"Including you." She leaned over and gave him a hearty buss on the cheek. *Especially you*, she thought with surprise. Especially when you sit there so quiet and at home. When you don't pressure me to give more than I can. When you don't take over and run everything your way. If only we could be like this all the time, I could love you fully, without reservation. The ice storm had isolated them, removed them in time and space, from all the tensions that normally disturbed their accord and she was happy to dwell in that peaceful center with him for as long as it lasted.

They finished eating in contented silence, then settled down on the sleeping bag for the evening. "It's kind of fun to be marooned," Susan commented lazily, swirling the wine around her cup and studying the ripples. "It reminds me of the snow days we got off from school when I was a kid. We'd bake cookies and play games all day."

She sat up, eyes shining as if she were still that little kid. "Do you want to play a game? I have one here. It's a communication game that we sometimes play in social psychology." This was their chance, she thought hopefully. They could pretend it was a game and be safe in their pretense, but they would still be talking.

"Sure," Nick agreed indulgently. "I'm game."

Susan groaned and punched him on the arm. She pulled a box off a shelf. "It's called the Ungame. It's a noncompetitive game—no one wins or loses. You just roll the dice and move around the board asking questions. Oh, and you're not allowed to comment on people's answers, you're just supposed to listen. I'll start." She set up the board, rolled the dice, and landed on a Tell It Like It Is square. She laughed when she read the card she drew. "Are you ready? You have to answer this. 'What advice would you give a young bride?'"

"I think the cards have been stacked," he protested.

"You have to answer. And you have to answer seriously, Nick. Not just jokes," she added when she saw the mischievous expression on his face.

"All right." He took a minute to think about it, then began. "I would tell a young bride that she should remember that men are just as vulnerable as women, that men need love and that men can be hurt even if they pretend they can't."

She studied him, wondering a little uneasily if he was talking about himself, about them. Already she was beginning to question the wisdom of playing this game. Maybe they would find out things they didn't want to know. "Now it's your turn," is all she said.

He rolled the dice, moved his marker around the board and drew a card. "'Share something that you fear.'"

"I fear death," she said with a shudder. She thought of her father and quickly drew another card but the card wouldn't let her escape the dark vision that had flashed into her mind. "'If you were told you only had one week to live how would you spend it?'"

"With you, my love, with you." His voice was soft and caressing. She was too young to be thinking of death, he thought. "Sleeping with you, touching you, laughing with you, looking at you."

He looked at her now until she grew uncomfortable and tried to hand him the dice.

He laughed gently and continued his answer. "You have the power to kill me . . . or cure me. See. Feel what you do to me," he said, moving closer to her and putting his arms around her. He took her hand and placed it on his heart. She could feel it pounding even through the thickness of his flannel shirt and wool sweater.

"And see what you do to me." The golden specks in his brown eyes glinted in the flickering candlelight. Fool's gold or buried treasure? she wondered.

He pushed the game aside and pulled her down beside him. There was none of the desperate urgency that had recently characterized their lovemaking. This time was different. It was a "laying on of hands," a healing. Gentle. Slow.

"I've never met anyone like you before," Susan whispered as she relaxed in his arms and pressed light kisses to his lips.

Nick buried his hands in her hair, feeling the soft curls twine around his fingers.

"You delight me . . . and seduce me . . . and unnerve me." Her voice was low and husky.

"Ah, Susie Q."

They fell asleep in each other's arms, oblivious to the chill in the room and the hard floor beneath them.

They slept soundly until they were abruptly awakened by a loud perfunctory knock. "Security," a young male announced as he opened the door.

Totally disoriented, Susan sat up and shook her head, trying to make sense of where she was and what was going on. The stunned look on the security guard's face must have mirrored her own.

"I beg your pardon," the young man stammered, mortified at the illicit scene he'd discovered. The lights, which had come on in the early-morning hours as the work crews restored the power lines, illuminated with cinematic clarity the guttered candles, the empty wine bottle, the flaky bread crumbs, and the man and woman. The heat had also come on during the night and, in their sleep, Nick and Susan had kicked away the sleeping bag. Nick was totally naked, lying on his stomach, and Susan only had on Nick's flannel shirt. "I didn't know anyone was here. I was just going to turn off the lights." He backed out of the door, red-faced. He hurried away, eager to escape the embarrassment of the whole situation, but before he got to the stairs, his training reasserted itself. A strange couple in a faculty office could not go uninvestigated. Jaw set with determination, he turned back to do his duty.

The appearance of the security guard had, in an instant, destroyed the precious harmony that Nick and Susan had found in the night. She sat, head buried in her hands, too sick at heart to move. Nick lay turned toward her, futilely searching for words to make it all right.

The door opened again and the security guard stepped into the room, more aggressively this time. "Could I see some ID?" he asked, as wooden and professional as a seasoned cop.

Part of her wanted to laugh at the absurdity of it all, part of her wanted to scream with frustration. Instead she got up, as emotionless as the young man, to get her purse. The flannel shirt was long enough for modesty but not long enough to hide the highly visible yellowish-purple bruise running the length of her thigh. There was not much point in being coy at this juncture; nevertheless, she found herself offering an explanation. "This is my office," she said as she hunted through her wallet for her picture identification card. "I couldn't make it home last night because of the ice. I fell." She gestured to her leg. "My husband," she pointed to Nick, "this is my husband—was concerned and came in to see if I was all right."

The security guard made no comment. He just looked hard at the picture, hard at her. "Professor Harkness," he said as if he was going to make sure he remembered the name. "Sorry to have bothered you."

When he left, Susan turned around and faced Nick who was sitting up with the sleeping bag draped around him like a toga. He could see the withdrawal in her eyes. Damn, damn, damn, he swore to himself. Why can't they leave us alone?

11

THEY WERE NEARLY HALFWAY through spring semester and Susan still hadn't taught the section on marriage and the family in her introductory class. She had been putting it off although she had ample textbook knowledge, in fact, years and years of textbook knowledge. She knew all the theories, but it turned out that her expertise left something to be desired when it came to the practicalities.

She couldn't skip the section. The three professors in the department had agreed to cover certain topics in their introductory classes and marriage and family was one of them. So now she stood in front of the class, struggling for words. What could she possibly tell these nineteen-year-olds to prepare them for marriage? At nineteen, everything seems so simple. You love each other, you get married and it all works out. Other people get divorced, but not you. Never you. You are smarter than that. Or more reasonable. Or more in love. You vow to try harder.

She cleared her throat and began to lecture. "When people marry, they enter into a contract. I know that sounds very legalistic and unromantic," she said, anticipating the objections of her students, "but it is a social fact. When couples marry, regardless of their feelings, they are bound by the laws of the state.

"In addition to the marriage contract of the state, it is possible for couples to draw up personal marriage contracts. Increasingly sociologists and marriage counselors are recommending that couples thinking of getting married prepare their own contracts. The contract forces couples to talk about how they feel about each other, money, careers, homes, children, sex and household chores, in short, all the things they will have to deal with in their marriage."

"Excuse me, Dr. Harkness." Bill McKenzie looked up from the notes he was scribbling and raised his hand. He was a bright, sarcastic student who dressed in torn jeans and a series of presumably secondhand bowling shirts since each one was embroidered with a different name. "Sex and household chores," he repeated. "Is that one category or two?"

"Two," she replied dryly.

"Two, thank you." He made a great show of correcting his notes. "You were recently married, weren't you?" he continued. "To the guy who gave the school a million bucks?"

She took a deep breath in preparation of what was coming. "Yes, I was."

"Did you and your husband draw up a marriage contract before you got married?"

She studied him warily. All the students were alert, waiting for the answer. If only they were this attentive when she was lecturing about sociological methodology. "No, we didn't," she said, "but we should have."

That was all she would say about the matter. In self-defense, she shifted the focus of her lecture and nearly put the class to sleep with a series of facts and figures on marriage patterns around the world. "In contrast to the Saxons of Transylvania, the Limbu people of Nepal . . ."

After class, she walked back to her office, depressed. She felt like a failure as a teacher and a wife. She was just another case of "do as I say, not as I do," one more example of adult hypocrisy. She had even lied to herself. She knew very well what she should have told her students. She should have told them that she loved her husband. Yes, she should have used the words. Stopped hiding. She loved her husband, but she felt as if she was competing against him. They were like the tortoise and the hare. He ran circles around her and the only way she could survive was to withdraw into a shell, hoping that it was hard enough to protect her.

When Richard walked into her office at one-thirty to suggest going off campus for a late lunch, she was more than ready to go with him.

"So how is the great man?" he asked when they were seated at a little Middle Eastern restaurant a few blocks away.

"Nick?"

"Who else? What would lunch be without at least one mention of him?"

"He's fine, busy working on the house." She stuck to a guarded factual report. "One day we're without water, the next day, we're without electricity. I'll be glad when it's all done."

"I was in The Hungry Mind bookstore the other day and saw your book. How is it doing?"

Susan brightened at the question. No one at school asked about her book and she hesitated to talk to Nick about it. "I talked to my publisher and she said reviews are starting to come out. I'm scared to death. I have nightmares of being publicly panned in the *Social Psychology Quarterly.* 'This woman is a fraud. Off with her head!'"

"It's a great book. Your research is as solid as the Rock of Gibraltar."

"Didn't I read that the Rock of Gibraltar was slowly sliding into the sea? Continental drift, or something?" She smiled at him shaking his head at her. "Oh, I know it's good, I do, thanks in part to you and your help on it, but you know that I stepped on a few toes. The reviews will depend on who is doing the reviewing."

The waitress brought them their falafels, juice dripping from the ends of the pita bread. "So far, I've been lucky," she said, reaching for an extra napkin. "My editor says the reviews she's seen have been positive. She's promised to send me copies. I'll show them to you as soon as I get them."

They fell silent while they ate their lunch, hunger driving out conversation. When they were finished, Susan picked up where she had left off. "Did I tell you that I got a nice letter from my dissertation supervisor, saying that he had nominated *Men and Women at Work* for the Social Psychology Association's George Herbert Mead award? The meetings are in Chicago next month. Are you going?"

"Yes. I'll drive if you want to come with me."

She detected the nervousness beneath the casual invitation. Richard was still car-shy since the accident. She nodded. "I'll be so excited and nervous that I'll need you for moral support. The problem is that all of this might be too late for tenure. Timing is so important and I got slowed down when my father died."

"Have you heard anything about tenure yet?" he asked. "FTP is meeting round the clock, it seems."

"Nothing. I don't know how much longer I can stand the suspense."

"You shouldn't have any trouble, Susan. If they turn you down, I'll resign and make such a fuss that they'll hire you back just to shut me up."

She would never allow him to make such an extravagant gesture, but she was touched by it anyway. "How are you doing?" she asked. "I don't think I've had two minutes alone with you this term."

"I've missed you," he said, "all the movies we saw together, drinks Friday night after work, the walks around the lake."

This burst of nostalgia was unlike Richard. Something must be wrong.

He fiddled with his silverware. "Of course, it's different now that you're married."

"I still care about you," she said impulsively. He looked so bereft that she took his hand in hers. "You're a good friend, Richard, and marriage doesn't change that for me."

"Would Nick agree?"

"He doesn't have anything to say about it," she answered, her chin thrust out determinedly. "It's my life and I choose my own friends." She didn't want to talk about Nick any more than Richard did. "How's Michelle?"

Richard's eyes clouded. "We're not going together anymore. She's dating a doctor she met while she was in the hospital."

"Oh, Richard, how awful! When did this happen?"

"A couple of weeks ago."

"A couple of weeks! Why didn't you tell me sooner?"

"I didn't want to bother you, tenure, newly wed, and all that."

"Don't be an idiot."

They stayed long after lunch drinking coffee and talking until Susan glanced at her watch. "It's nearly five o'clock," she exclaimed. "I've got to get home. Nick will start to worry."

"You're more married than you think."

She leaned over and kissed him on the cheek. "Maybe I am," she said ruefully, "but call me if you need me. I mean it. Promise?"

"Promise."

Susan's wool-lined Burberry flapped open at the knees as she walked home. March was blowing in like a lion, but there was a mildness in the air that promised spring. The melting snow left puddles on the sidewalks that froze at night and thawed again during the day in an ever shrinking cycle and the bare tree branches were growing thicker, pregnant with buds and blossoms.

Her footsteps slowed the closer she got to the house. She and Nick were becoming polite strangers sharing temporary living quarters, taking turns cooking, cleaning and shopping, keeping each other posted on their general whereabouts, exchanging family news, and making sure they put the cap back on the tube of toothpaste. They were the model of decorum. They were both holding back, afraid to upset the delicate balance of their relationship, but they were losing something indefinably precious in the process. Either way they lost and Susan could not see any way out of it.

A curtain moved in the dining-room window as she walked up the front steps into the porch. That's odd, she thought. Was Nick watching for her? She turned the doorknob. It was locked. That was strange, too. He never locked the door when he was at home. She pulled her keys out of her purse and unlocked the door. With the curtains drawn, the dining room and living room were quite dark. "Nick?" she called a bit nervously as she shut the door behind her.

"Surprise!" The lights flashed on and fifteen Humboldt professors stood there with champagne glasses in their hands. Nick was over by the light switch, standing under the wooden arch that separated the two rooms. Over his head was a banner that looked as though it had been hastily made out of grocery bags. "Congratulations!" it read in big red magic-marker letters.

For a moment, Susan was unable to speak because her heart was racing so furiously from the shock. "What's going on?" she finally asked the grinning faces.

Nick came forward and gave her a big hug. She hadn't seen him so happy since their wedding day. "Dean Anderson called this afternoon with the wonderful news. You've been granted tenure!"

The dean was standing by the card table, which Nick had moved into the dining room and loaded down with food. "Congratulations, Susan," he said, coming over to shake her hand. Everyone else raised their glasses in a toast and congratulations rang through the house.

Nick hugged her again and handed her a glass of champagne. "Where did all these people come from?" she asked, still in a daze.

"Both the dean and I tried to reach you at your office to tell you the good news. Don't you usually have office hours on Friday afternoon?" He was so excited that he didn't wait for an answer. "I got on the phone and called everyone I could think of to come over and celebrate. A friend of mine who is a caterer managed to throw some food together at the last minute and *voilà*, a party."

"It's certainly a surprise."

"Susan!" Molly tugged on her arm. "Isn't it wonderful? I'm so happy for you." She, too, gave her a big hug. "Wasn't it sweet of Nick to organize the party?"

Susan was prevented from answering by Fred Harrison who materialized by her side. "Congratulations," he said in a booming voice. "The vote was unanimous."

"Thank you." She extended her hand for a handshake, but he had already turned to face Nick and Susan found herself staring at his back.

"Nick, fine party," Fred said to him, shaking his hand. "Say, I never got to thank you for your impressive donation to Humboldt. We were talking about your generosity just the other day during an FTP meeting. Most appreciated, most appreciated."

Susan felt the color fading from her cheeks. Fred's voice carried to every corner of the room and several people glanced speculatively in their direction. One of them was Will Lambert.

"Who invited Lambert here?" Molly gasped under her breath. Susan had told her about the suspicions she and Nick had about Will and Molly, playing detective, had talked to some of her sources and confirmed their suspicions. "I bet he tagged along with Herman," she said, nodding in the direction of Susan's chairman. "You know Herman is too polite to tell him to get lost."

"And now there will be a new batch of rumors," Susan said grimly. "He'll tell everyone that Nick's money bought me tenure."

"You deserve tenure."

"You know that and I know it. How many others do?"

"FTP knew it and that's who counts."

"Did they? I wonder."

"Don't let Fred Harrison's big mouth and Will's scheming ruin it for you."

Susan tried to follow Molly's advice as she circulated among the guests, but she couldn't help wondering what her well-wishers were thinking.

"Congratulations, Susan," Will said with a smirk on his face. "You'd better watch out, Herman." He licked his finger and held it up as if testing the direction of the wind. "Today tenure, tomorrow the chair."

"Better the chair than the boot," she returned pleasantly with all the control she could muster. "It's a pity you won't be with us any longer. Good luck on your job search." She licked her finger and mimicked his gesture. "Today Humboldt, tomorrow humbled." Then she turned and walked away with her head held high.

People drifted in and out all evening. Susan was hoarse from talking by the end of the night. Finally it was just she and Nick, sitting on two folding chairs in the midst of the party debris, ashtrays full of stubbed cigarettes, champagne glasses everywhere, bits of cheese turning hard around the edges, cake crumbs scattered on the floor, the congratulations banner hanging by one end.

Nick surveyed the damage with an air of satisfaction. As far as he was concerned, the greater the mess, the better the party. "A lot of people showed up, given such short notice," he observed.

Susan nodded. After a moment, she said, "Richard wasn't here. I should tell him about my tenure."

"I tried to call him this afternoon both at his office and apartment, but he wasn't in." As soon as Nick said the words, he put two and two together, his breath painfully sticking in his chest.

"I'll go call him. He and Michelle just broke up and he needs some good news. This will make him happy."

Nick got to his feet. "I'll clean up," he said in short, clipped tones.

Susan headed upstairs. "I'll be down to help you as soon as I've talked to Richard and changed my clothes."

As Nick put the leftover food into the refrigerator, he could hear her talking on the upstairs phone. The elation he had felt ever since the dean had called with the news ebbed away, leaving him suddenly tired. He had thought that Susan would be as happy as he was about the tenure decision, but she didn't seem pleased at all. He had hoped that with the tenure question settled, they could get on with their lives, make a real marriage out of this sham they were living, but everything was going wrong.

He had nearly everything in the dishwasher by the time she came downstairs. "Sorry, I took longer than I expected. What's left? What can I do?"

"You can tell me what's wrong," he said, facing her squarely. "I thought you would be happy about tenure. Perhaps the party was a bad idea. If so, I'm sorry. I thought you would want to celebrate. I wanted to celebrate. Maybe I got carried away." He stopped, hearing the rush of the words that poured out of him as fast and furiously as water from a crumbling dam. "Susan, what is wrong with us? We are drifting farther apart, not closer together. I thought you were worried about tenure and I've tried not to make demands. What more can I do?"

"You've done quite enough already!"

He was taken back at the anger in her voice.

"What does the tenure decision mean after all the politics and manipulations of the past four months?" she burst out. "How did your million-dollar contribution affect the decision? Did the committee even bother to look at my work or were they too busy figuring out how to thank you? 'I know, let's give tenure to his wife.'"

She strode up and down the kitchen, propelled by the force of her emotions. "Not only have you rushed me into marriage, taken over my house, and completely changed my personal life, but you have usurped my professional life as well. I hear about my tenure decision from you, secondhand. No, wait." She mentally reviewed the number of people who had been at the party. "I hear about tenure thirty-secondhand! Even Will Lambert hears about it before I do! I have become an insignificant factor in my own career."

"I never intended—"

"The road to hell is paved with good intentions."

Nick sat in the kitchen for an hour after she had gone to bed, thinking and drinking flat champagne. He had been so caught up loving her and wanting their marriage to succeed that he had not stopped to really think about her life at Humboldt. He had to admit that he had sometimes regarded her job as an intrusion into their life together. He wanted her to be as free as he was. He particularly wanted her to be free of Richard. At Humboldt, she shared an important part of her life with Richard from which he was forever excluded. He didn't want to become a sociologist to replace Richard as a confidant and he knew she would never resign from her job. He couldn't see any way out.

Susan was lying on her side on the far side of the bed when he went upstairs. He got undressed and crawled into his side of the bed, turning his back to her. They were like a pair of marble bookends, set rigidly in place, holding nothing together. He assumed that she was as sleepless as he, but neither of them made a sound.

He stared at the wall for what seemed like hours, listening for her breathing, for any sign of her presence, for there would be only one thing worse than having her lie in the same bed separated from him by anger, and that would be not to have her lying there beside him at all.

12

SUSAN WOKE UP in the morning with an emotional hangover. She pulled the pillow over her head and wished she were somewhere else in a different time. Paris in the 1890s, the banquet years, would be nice. Anywhere but here with Nick after last night's scene. She peeked in his direction through the pillowcase's lace edging and discovered he was not in bed. She breathed a sigh of relief although she was only postponing the inevitable confrontation. Should she apologize? But she meant what she had said. He hadn't meant to rob her of the joy of receiving tenure. But he had. But, but, but.

When she went downstairs, he was sitting in the kitchen reading the newspaper. "There's coffee in the thermos," he said without looking up. He steeled himself not to speak further.

She poured herself a cup and sat down. What do you do when someone gives you a gift you don't want? "Thank you for the party." The words took effort. "You went to a lot of trouble." She knew it was not enough, but it was the best she could do.

"Don't mention it."

He was so unusually remote that she found that she could do better after all. "I'm sorry I lashed out at you."

Finally he looked at her. The crow's feet at the corner of his eyes were more deeply set than they had been yesterday. She wanted to reach out to smooth away the lines. Touching him would comfort him, perhaps even comfort her, but the solace would be illusory. Afterward, they would feel more empty and alone than before. She didn't move.

"Giving Humboldt a million dollars was an extravagant gesture done partly to please you, partly to tease you, and partly to entrap you, but never to hurt you."

"I know." But both of them were aware there was no solace in that knowledge.

"As for the house, I can't stop now with everything torn apart."

"I know."

There was a long silence as each of them came to the same sad conclusion.

"Then there's nothing to be done?" he asked woodenly.

"No, I guess not." She couldn't look him in the eyes or she would burst into tears. Instead she sat there, staring down at the tablecloth, miserable and stuck.

"I'm sorry."

"So am I."

And so, as spring progressed, in contrast to the earth, which was slowly heating under the strengthening sun, relations between them cooled until their marriage was a study in cryogenics. Nick no longer warmed Susan with his breath as he whispered his love along the length of her body, no longer covered her shivering limbs with his lean muscular frame. They never talked about the past or the future. They worked long hours and fell into bed exhausted, each uttering an individual prayer for merciful sleep.

The Social Psychology meetings were March 26th through the 29th. Susan had told Nick that she was going, but she had been reluctant to tell him the particulars. It didn't take a social psychologist to be able to predict his reaction. Every day for a week before the meetings, she waited for an opening to talk to him about it, but somehow the opportunity never came. She didn't dare admit the truth, which was that she couldn't bear the thought of arguing openly with him. It hurt too much. So she delayed telling him until the last possible moment.

The day she was to leave, she brought it up at breakfast. "I'm leaving for Chicago this morning," she announced offhandedly.

"What?" Nick looked totally nonplussed.

"The Social Psychology meetings, remember? I told you about them sometime ago." She paused and then added rather guiltily, "I probably should have reminded you, but we don't have anything special planned for the next few days, so I didn't think it would make any difference. I didn't want to bother you."

"Bother me," Nick repeated numbly. An awkward silence followed. "Do you need a ride to the airport?" he finally asked.

She took the plunge. "No, Richard is picking me up. We're driving down together."

"You're what?"

"Richard is going to the meetings, too. He's driving and I'm riding along," she repeated casually as if she thought he just hadn't heard what she had said even though she knew differently.

"Is anyone else going with you?"

"No, just the two of us."

"You never mentioned that before."

"Didn't I? I guess I didn't think it was important." Her tone of voice was getting considerably less casual.

"Well, I think it's damned important."

"Well, it shouldn't be."

"Well, it is."

They glared at each other, abruptly angry at each other for forcing the issue, angry that they were reduced to having such a stupid quarrel that was no less strongly felt for all of its stupidity.

"Are you going to be staying at the same hotel?" Nick continued, compelled to know the worst.

"Of course. The conference is at the downtown Hilton." She pleated her napkin with nervous fingers.

"Sleeping together?"

She shot him a scornful look and refused to answer such an insulting question.

"I don't want you to go," he stated flatly, making his position perfectly clear. He knew he was risking her rebellion but the jealousy and hurt he felt overwhelmed his better judgment. "I forbid you to go!" He knew it was a mistake as soon as the words were out of his mouth. Susan was not some wayward girl who would thrill to this display of dominant masculine authority.

"I'm giving a paper and my book has been nominated for an award," she explained carefully, eyes flashing with a fury she did not allow herself to express. She would not sink to his level. "I have to go. No, it's more than that. I want to go. No, that's not it, either. Oh, hell! I'm going. I'm just going!"

"Then I'm coming, too."

"No, you're not."

"Why not? If you and Richard are just good friends as you've maintained ad nauseam, why can't I come?"

"I'll be busy and I don't want to be distracted." She faced him defiantly. "I need time away from you, Nick. Time to think."

His stomach clenched with tension. "Think about what?"

"About whether this is going to work. Our marriage."

"I think you've already decided," he said, shoving his chair back with such physical force that Susan jumped. "You've already judged." Suddenly he was tired, as if standing up had sapped him of all his energy. So exhausted that all the fight drained out of him. "You don't have to go away to think. I'm leaving," he said in a defeated voice. "After all, it is your house, isn't it? Your friends. Your work. Your life. There's no room for me here."

"Nick," she called after him, her anger evaporating into alarm. What had she done? "Wait!" But he didn't turn around; he just slammed the door behind him and kept on going.

"WHAT'S WRONG?" Richard asked after one look at her red eyes when he came to pick her up.

"Nick and I had a fight," she replied, the tears spilling over. "He walked out, and I don't think he's coming back."

"There, there," he murmured, patting her back while surreptitiously glancing at his watch. After a brief interval, he said, "Uh, we'd better get going. It's a long drive. Have you got everything?"

"I don't know." She hovered indecisively by her suitcase. Should she go or stay?"

"Susan, oh, Susan, are you in there?" Richard snapped his fingers in front of her face as if to wake her from a deep trance. "George Herbert Mead awaits us."

She shook off her uncertainty. "All right, I'm coming." She locked the door behind her and turned her back on the house, Nick, and all her problems, but no sooner had she gotten into the car, than she said in a panic, "Wait a minute, I'll be right back," and ran into the house.

Once inside, she sat down at Nick's dining-room table and quickly wrote him a note. She could have spent hours composing that note but, aware that Richard was impatiently waiting in the car, she only had time to leave him the address and phone number of the hotel where she would be staying. "I'll be back Sunday evening," she scribbled. Love, Susan? Hope you will be here when I return? Please come back to me?

Outside, Richard was honking his horn.

With a frustrated exclamation, she signed the note simply, "Susie Q," and hurried out to the car.

As soon as they walked into the Hilton, Susan ran into her dissertation supervisor who whisked her off for a drink to catch up on professional gossip. She was surprised to discover that she knew at least half of the people milling around the bar from her graduate school days at the University of Chicago.

"Hey, Susan, read your book. Good work!"

"We're staying in Room 306. Come on up after the reception. We're having a party."

"Are you going to the SWS meeting? Try to make it. We're voting on some important bylaws."

"I just talked to the University of Chicago Press representative and he's looking for you. He said something about an interview about your research on WGN."

"Susan, is that a wedding ring you're wearing? I want to hear all about it!"

Smoke and conversations whirled around her as she sat at the bar, sandwiched in between her portly supervisor and the Association president who were arguing about licensing social psychologists. Her supervisor jabbed the air with an unlit cigar, all soggy and chewed flat on one end, to illustrate his point while the president pounded the table with his fist. The sweating Scotch and soda glasses jumped and vibrated and shed more sweat as the two men articulated and gesticulated to their hearts' content.

Susan listened with equal parts fascination and boredom. What would Nick make of it all? she wondered. He would probably quote something, she decided, a smile automatically appearing on her lips. She could almost hear him, his voice low and mocking. He would lean over and whisper in her ear, his breath soft and warm against her cheek, "it is a tale told by an idiot, full of sound and fury, signifying nothing." He would keep his face straight, but she would be unable to restrain a laugh as embarrassing as an empty stomach growling during a silent prayer in church. God, she missed him already. Nicky, Nicky, what am I going to do about you?

A vaguely familiar male voice interrupted her reverie. "May I join you?"

She looked up and there was the legendary Professor Tom Sexton standing by the table. He had joined the University of Chicago faculty just a year before she graduated so she hadn't taken any classes with him but she had met him in passing and she had certainly heard about him. The sociology Graduate Women Caucus seemed to spend as much time analyzing the myriad attractions of Dr. Ton o' Sex, as he was quickly nicknamed, as it did student policies. If Susan recalled correctly, a random sample of the women polled at one meeting had listed, in order, a nice rear, deep blue eyes, thick curly blond hair and a devastating smile as his finest features. At the following meeting, after being reminded by one of the more political members of the group that judging a person solely by physical appearance was inherently unjust, they had added his brilliance as a sociologist to the list. This was fine until the next meeting when judging people by their intelligence was also called into question. After this philosophical challenge, the group ceased all discussion of Dr. Sexton; he proved to be much too complicated an issue for the caucus to handle. Nevertheless, whenever two or three women gathered together in the halls, talk of Tom Sexton was sure to be heard.

"Certainly, come sit down." Susan's supervisor moved his chair over so Tom could slide another chair in beside Susan. "I can't remember. Do you know Susan Harkness?"

"Yes, we've met," Tom replied with the famous devastating smile as he shook her hand. "But I didn't get to know her as well as I would have liked to."

A charming man, Susan thought bemusedly as she withdrew her hand from his gently caressing grasp. So far the blue eyes, blond hair and smile checked out. Should she verify the rest of the data?

"I use your book in my undergraduate sociology of work class," he told her.

"Then I owe you a drink for royalties paid," she replied and looked for the waiter so she could buy a round of drinks for herself and the three men at the table.

As she flagged the harried man down, she glanced around the bar and realized that people in every corner of the room were watching her. For a brief paranoid moment, she wondered if the old Humboldt rumors had reached the convention and she was once again the object of scandal, but sanity quickly prevailed. She looked at her companions—the president of the association, her supervisor who was a past-president, and the legendary Tom Sexton—and understood. She was at the Power Table! She nearly laughed out loud.

"I like a woman who is strong enough to buy a man a drink," Tom said softly in her direction.

"'I am woman. Hear me roar,'" she quipped, a little giddy from all the attention, but instead of a responsive glimmer of humor, he merely looked puzzled. Mentally shrugging her shoulders, she dropped it and said, "What are you working on these days?" It was the right thing to say.

Blue is supposed to be a cool color but Tom Sexton's eyes sparkled with blue heat when he was enthusiastic and Susan had to force herself to pay attention to the research he was describing rather than simply staring into his eyes and getting lost. No man had the right to have such beautiful eyes, she thought, and to be so bright, for as he talked, he proved to be as brilliant as the women students had said. Four out of five, she enumerated. Four out of five ain't bad.

She was surprised to find herself attracted to Tom Sexton. She had been so focused on Nick that she had forgotten other men existed for purposes other than tenure, promotion and publication. She bit her lip, simultaneously excited and guilty about her excitement. What would Tom Sexton be like in bed? she wondered.

It was as if she had spoken her thoughts out loud. Immediately he broke off in the middle of his sentence. Research forgotten, they sat there, looking at each other, breathing unevenly, confused and tantalized.

Susan started to panic as the two older men beside them began to notice their strained silence.

"Is something the matter?" her supervisor asked, always forthright to the point of bluntness.

"No. Ah, an old friend of mine just walked in," she improvised, waving at a group of people who were coming through the door. At least two of them turned around to see if she was waving to someone behind them, another pointed at his chest with a quizzical expression on his face as if to say "Who? Me?" and four total strangers waved enthusiastically back at her. "I haven't seen her since the meetings last year. If you'll excuse me?" She made her escape.

Safely locked away in the privacy of her room, she sat down in an easy chair to take stock of the situation. "Now, reason it out," she told herself, falling back on her academic training. She composed herself, hands folded neatly on her lap, knees and feet together like a proper lady, shoulders relaxed, deep breaths in and out, mind receptive. "I am a tranquil harbor in a stormy sea," she intoned hypnotically, calming herself down so she could think clearly. "I am a springtime meadow. I am a brook trickling over smooth rocks. I am..." She paused, searching for harmonious essence and in that brief unguarded moment, Nick folded back into her being and spoke. "*A total fruitcake!*"

"Aaarg!" She jumped up and started to pace, propelled by frustrated energy. Tom Sexton would have been crushed to learn that he had remained in her thoughts for precisely eleven seconds before being superceded.

"*Sugar.*" Nick's voice, teasing and seductive, sounded in her head, leading her thoughts home.

"Maybe I should forget my pride. Why be upset about the tenure decision?" she argued with herself as she steered around the coffee table and easy chair. "I got it and that's all that counts."

"*Honey.*"

She went into the bathroom and confronted herself in the mirror. "And what does it matter about the house? It's our home now and Nick is transforming it into something beautiful and comfortable, something it never was before, something I could never have done on my own." She went back into the bedroom, pacing back and forth like a tiger penned in a cage too small for its size. "Why should Nick and I fight about Richard? Our relationship has peaked and subsided into an undemanding friendship. Why jeopardize my marriage for that?"

"Sweetie pie, my pie, My Tai. Tie one on and we'll dance till dawn." She couldn't get Nick's voice out of her mind.

She picked up the phone on the bedside stand to call him but immediately slammed down the receiver again. "On the other hand, why should I have to compromise?" she muttered rebelliously, stifling Nick's voice. "Why must I sacrifice ambition for love? He is asking me to pay a high price for marriage. He's overwhelmingly generous, but his generosity doesn't cost him anything. He is still the same man before and after. I'm the one being asked to change, to accept."

But for all this fine resolve, she could not entirely silence a persistent underlying fear, a fear so powerful she could not say it out loud. What if he's not there when I go home? What if he's left for good? How could I live without him?

After an hour of restless solitary confinement, she was no closer to knowing what to do about Nick and was relieved when Richard knocked on her door to pick her up for the opening reception.

The ballroom was so jammed with people when they walked in that it took them fifteen minutes of politely and finally not-so-politely pushing to reach the bar and the hors d'oeuvre table, which bore only crumbs as a clue to what had been initially offered.

"Whew," Susan breathed as they maneuvered over to a relatively unoccupied corner, drinks held high to avoid spilling. "I'm not quite sure, but I think I had intimate physical relationships with at least a half dozen people on the way in here."

"I'm only sorry I wasn't one of them," Tom Sexton said behind her.

It was exactly the kind of lighthearted scandalous thing Nick would have said. She turned, laughing and ready to banter something equally nonsensical back.

Richard saw her mistake before she did and dug her sharply in the ribs with his elbow. "Susan, he means it!" he hissed in her ear.

Swallowing her words, she stopped, looked at Tom, and realized that Richard was right. Something about the expression in Tom's blue eyes and the way he stood next to her, just a little bit closer than he should have, proclaimed his intention to the entire ballroom. He was not joking.

Stepping back to give herself more distance, she introduced the two men and steered the conversation to safe academic ground. It was not easygoing. Tom clearly regarded Richard as a third wheel and kept ignoring him. Richard, undaunted, stuck to Susan's side like super glue. Eventually they finished their drinks, but Susan noticed that neither of the men volunteered to go replenish them and thus leave the field open to the other one. She also discovered that she was having a good time. Richard and Tom reminded her of two greedy little boys eyeing the last piece of cake on the plate. She was surprised by their attention, flattered by it, and finally, amused by it. After an hour of uninspired shoptalk, Tom got discouraged and excused himself.

"Why was he coming on to you?" Richard said indignantly as they watched him walk away. "You're a married woman."

"I may be married, but I'm not dead yet. Besides, since when have you become so protective of moral virtue?" she asked, her eyes still on the departing Tom. The graduate women had been right about the derriere. Five out of five. Bingo.

"I wouldn't like to see Nick get hurt."

She focused back on Richard. "I thought you hated Nick," she said with astonishment.

"He has a certain style I admire," Richard admitted, then quickly closed the subject. "Are you going to be okay if I leave? I want to mingle a bit."

"I think I can survive without you," she replied dryly. "See you later." Then she, too, left the quiet corner to seek out some graduate school colleagues who were laughing and talking loudly by the bar, an impromptu reunion that lasted until two in the morning.

Susan spent the next two days totally immersed in the conference, surrounded by other social psychologists who were eager to discuss the latest research and exchange information over endless cups of strong black coffee. Encapsulated in a small teaching college, she had forgotten that a world existed that was more familiar with her field and her accomplishments. Instead of having to struggle to be accepted by the Humboldt Faculty Tenure and Promotions Committee, a group that knew little about social psychology and who viewed newcomers with caution, she was welcomed by her discipline's leaders. Enthusiastically endorsed by her dissertation supervisor, the president of the association asked her to collaborate on a textbook he was writing, a textbook that was sure to be profitable to both publisher and authors. Her academic future was ensured.

In addition, there was standing room only for her paper presentation. She had a moment's qualm when she saw that the social psychologists whose work she had criticized in *Men and Women at Work* were there in full force. And sure enough, as soon as she was finished, one of them jumped up and attacked her research in a diatribe that would have shattered her a few months ago. "Full of sound and fury," she reminded herself with an inward smile, "signifying nothing," and proceeded to coolly demolish his objections. Her rebuttal was seconded by more heated defense by the supporters of her work, including Tom Sexton, followed in turn by more attacks from the opposition. It was vicious; it was loud; it was unruly. Everyone agreed that it was the best session of the conference.

Susan was exhausted after her paper and excused herself from further revelry. As soon as she unlocked her hotel room door, she anxiously checked the message light on her phone. No light, no messages. Her triumph dimmed a bit. Why hadn't Nick called? She wanted to tell him about the conference; she wanted to tell him she missed him. Would he listen?

Steeling herself against the possibility of more angry words, she picked up the receiver and dialed their home number. The phone rang but there was no answer. She let it ring a half dozen times. Maybe he was on top of a stepladder changing a light bulb or putting in a ceiling. It would take him a while to answer. A dozen times. Maybe he was using one of his power tools and couldn't hear the phone. Two dozen times. Maybe he just wasn't there.

She hung up and was about to dial again in case she had accidentally phoned the wrong number when there was a knock at the door. She brushed away the tears that had begun to slowly form in the corners of her eyes and answered the door.

"May I?" Tom Sexton asked with a smile. He was holding a champagne bottle and two glasses. "I think a celebration is in order."

She considered turning him away but she didn't want to be rude. More truthfully, she had to admit that the prospect of listening to the phone ring in an empty house was too much to bear by herself. She needed some company.

"Sure, come in," she said.

When they were seated at the small round table by the window in a corner of the room, as far away from the bed as Susan could arrange it, Tom opened the champagne and poured them each a drink. "To your continued success." He raised his glass in a toast.

Susan clinked her glass with his. "Thank you." He was a nice man, she thought warmly.

"And to our continued relationship."

Little red warning lights went off in her head. "I didn't know we had a relationship," she said lightly.

"We're going to."

"What kind of relationship do you have in mind?"

"A sexual one."

"Oh, is that all?" She was beginning to get nettled at his casual assumption that she was a ready and willing sexual partner, one in a long line of graduate student conquests and conference one-night stands. Obviously his toast to *her* success had been mere subterfuge; he had really been toasting to *his* continued success!

"That's everything."

A jolt ran through her. Hadn't Nick said that very thing? But he had put it differently, had added something else. "No, it's not. Laughter and sex—that's everything, or so I'm told."

"What's laughter got to do with it?"

She should have know that he wouldn't understand. "You might as well ask what's love got to do with it," she murmured.

"Who said anything about love?" Tom visibly backed away at the mention of the *L* word.

"No one in this room."

He looked relieved, completely missing the note of mockery in Susan's voice. "Sex without emotional entanglements is the way to go," he asserted.

"Tell me, do you think sex without love is better than love without sex?" She thought of the past few weeks of celibacy between herself and Nick.

"Of course." He looked at her as if she was crazy for even considering the possibility.

"No, you're wrong." She didn't bother to explain. "And what about fidelity? Don't you care about being faithful to your wife?" She pointed to the gold band he wore on his left hand.

"Fidelity is a social construction. It's not natural. Besides I don't think that just pure sex counts."

"You have a strange accounting system." She took a deep draught of champagne.

"We've done enough talking now, don't you think?" Tom edged his chair closer to hers and started to stroke her arm.

"Aha! I think, therefore, I am." Nick, preserve me from unimaginative lovers like Tom Sexton.

She could see that he was taken back by the Descartes. It was a fairly safe bet that no woman he had made love to before had ever broken into philosophical announcements during his version of foreplay. After a brief pause, he leaned over and nuzzled her neck. He had apparently decided to ignore her breach of proper procedure.

"'And I y'am what I y'am what I y'am.'"

The Popeye was too much for him. He froze in place, as if he didn't want to disturb her precarious mental state with any sudden movements that might tip her over the edge.

"Yam: a starchy root," she continued with a giggle. "Poor Tom, I was rooting for you but you're much too starchy for me."

Slowly, ever so slowly, he drew back, got to his feet, and headed for the door.

"Don't you ever cut loose and have fun?" she asked curiously.

He swiveled around to glare at her. "Look, I'm not interested in having fun. I just wanted to go to bed with you."

"I'm sorry. I could never go to bed with a man who has the sense of humor of a mongoose."

Without another word, he marched to the door, wrenched it open and slammed it hard behind him.

Susan watched him go without regret for she had seen what the bedazzled women graduate students had failed to see. Tom Sexton was indeed gorgeous; he was a highly skilled sociologist; he was even seductive; but he had no playful streak, no sense of timing, and without those traits, he held no attraction for her. In fact, she realized that she could put it even more simply than that. *He wasn't Nick.*

She went to the phone and dialed again. Still no answer. Descartes notwithstanding, she resolutely avoided thinking. Instead she flipped on the television and mindlessly watched old movies for hour after hour into the long night. In the morning, she couldn't exactly remember what she had seen but she knew they must have been real tearjerkers because her eyes were all red and swollen.

She didn't see either Tom or Richard at breakfast. In fact, she had seen very little of Richard since the reception. When she ran into him the day before, he was so preoccupied with a striking female graduate student from the University of Minnesota that he scarcely noticed her. Michelle was apparently a discarded memory. His healing process was well on its way.

She wished she could shake her thoughts of Nick as easily. After several of the sessions she attended, she looked down at the notes she had taken, or thought she had taken, to discover that she had scribbled pages of doodles—Nick's name in embroidered scripts, hearts pierced with arrows, rockets shooting into space, a train going into a tunnel.

The culminating event was the conference awards banquet that night. There were a few sessions scheduled for the next morning, but anyone who got assigned that time period gloomily adjusted their expectations of attendance downward by a factor of ten. Susan sat through the dinner too excited to eat much, then through the long introductions of Association notables and the keynote speaker.

Finally the president got to the part she had been waiting for. "The winner of the George Herbert Mead Award for outstanding work by a young professional is—" He paused for dramatic effect, obviously a faithful viewer of the Academy Awards "—Dr. Susan Harkness, Humboldt College, Minneapolis, Minnesota!"

Taking a deep breath, she stood up and made her way to the podium amidst the applause. She made a brief thank-you speech, her eyes flicking over the crowd. There was Richard grinning broadly, sitting beside the graduate student. Throughout the audience, she could see former professors and fellow students, poking their dinner companions in the ribs and mouthing the words, I know her. Even Tom Sexton was smiling at her.

There was only one person missing, but his absence loomed so large that it cast a shadow over her gratification. She had wanted to bask in the glory alone, she reminded herself.

Her supervisor took her out for a drink after the banquet. "You know, you've changed," he said as they sat down.

"In what way?" she asked with surprise.

"You've matured intellectually. Your dissertation was solid, substantial work, but it wasn't particularly inspiring. The research you did on your own for the book, however, is fresh and thought-provoking. It goes far beyond your graduate work. What happened?"

"Teaching undergraduates, I suppose. There's nothing like teaching to clarify your muddled thinking. If you don't understand something, how can you explain it to your students? It is wonderful how much inspiration can be derived from thirty blank faces staring at you in a silent classroom!"

Her supervisor shook his head doubtfully. "You're wasting your time teaching at Humboldt. You should be doing more research. How many different classes do you teach a year anyway?"

"Six, three a term, no repeats."

"That's outrageous! We teach the same two a term with graduate student assistants to help with both teaching and research. I won't even ask about salary."

"That's the wisest course," she agreed, "although we are going to get a substantial increase this coming year.

We had a big donation," she paused before confessing, "from my husband."

"Send him my way, will you?"

"By the way," she added, following her train of thought, "I just received tenure."

Her supervisor set down his glass and studied her speculatively. "Before or after the donation?"

"After," she answered abruptly.

"You were lucky then."

"What do you mean?" She was astonished at his reaction. "I would have thought the opposite."

"You mustn't always seize on the easy answer or even the most likely one," her supervisor said, her teacher once again. "I started out teaching at a college like Humboldt—small and proud—and the tenure committees at these institutions..." He shook his head. "I swear the members of tenure committees are the most difficult and unpredictable faculty of all. You're lucky they didn't assume that you would drop out of academia to have babies and be supported by your rich husband. You're lucky they didn't deny you tenure just to prove their independence. Academics simultaneously scorn and crave money. Your husband set up some dangerous crosscurrents when he donated money to the college. It's fortunate you didn't get swept away."

"I never thought of it that way," she said slowly.

"Humboldt must be a better school than I thought. Nevertheless," he said, poking a finger at her, "I still think you should go to a research-oriented institution."

"No, thanks," Susan said with a smile. "I like where I am just fine." She downed the rest of her champagne and set the glass down with a decisive click. "Thank you."

"For what?"

"For being the straw that broke the camel's back," she said and impulsively leaned over and kissed him. "Now, if you'll excuse me, I have a plane to catch."

"That's another way you're changed," her supervisor observed. "You've gotten stronger, bolder and more mysterious all at the same time. You've grown into a fascinating woman, Susan Harkness."

"It's the company I've been keeping."

"It's good for you." He smiled indulgently as she stood up to go.

"You should meet my husband," she said, gathering up her purse and conference program. "You and he would get along just fine."

"Come visit us this summer during the blues festival," he called after her as she hurried off.

"We will." A big promise, she thought more soberly, for someone who doesn't even know if she still has a husband.

13

EVERY LIGHT IN THE HOUSE was burning brightly when Susan pulled up in a taxi at midnight. As she swung her legs out of the car, her arms filled with the entire inventory of red roses from the hotel's gift shop, she stepped into a white light that was as reassuring as a lighthouse beacon on a stormy night. Nick was home.

The cabdriver carried her suitcase onto the porch and chivalrously waited until she unlocked the door before leaving. He didn't look at the tip she had handed him before he got back into the car but when he did, he turned on the overhead light to make sure he was reading the numbers on the bill correctly. An intelligent man, he quickly figured it out. "Young love," he muttered to himself with a grin as he pocketed the money. "Ain't it grand?"

The house was completely silent when she let herself in and a little of her confidence slipped away. "Nick?" Her voice came out in a whisper. Her imagination, which had considerably enlivened her flight home with slow motion pictures of herself dressed in a long white gown and Nick naked from the waist up running barefoot toward each other in a daisy-filled field—never mind that it was still March in Minnesota—turned to less cheerful images. Every newspaper article she had ever read about fatal household accidents came back to her word by word, line by line—power tools, water, electricity, flames, falls. "Nick?" she called in a louder voice, starting up the stairs.

She found him in the study, sitting in her grandmother's rocking chair, her own favorite chair, clutching a glass of brandy. His face was lined with dark stubble as if he hadn't shaved since she left and there were dark circles under his eyes as if he hadn't slept, either. His skin, so warm with its brown hues that never faded even during the long winter, looked drawn and gray. With a great effort, he lifted his head and looked at her standing in the doorway. She nearly cried out at the dullness of his eyes, all sparkle and light extinguished. She had been wrong about the cost.

"Oh, Nick," she said as she crossed the room and knelt beside him, roses spilling into his lap. "I'm so sorry." She reached up and caressed his cheek, his beard rough against her fingertips. "Wait right here," she told him unnecessarily. He seemed incapable of movement.

She left the room, taking a few of the roses with her. In the bathroom, she turned on the water in the tub. She gently plucked the petals from their stems and scattered them in the water until the tub was a floating bed of roses.

Downstairs she gathered up every vase and empty mayonnaise jar she could find for the flowers. When she went back into the study, Nick hadn't stirred. She took the roses from his lap, brushing his mouth with one perfect unfurling bud. His lips parted slightly with the touch. Encouraged by his response, Susan traced the outline of his lips with the tip of her tongue and pressed soft kisses against his mouth. She could taste brandy and despair.

She pulled away to put the rest of the roses in water. When she was finished, there were nine vases and jars full, roses in the study, roses in the bathroom, roses in the bedroom, roses in every room of the house.

"Susan," Nick managed to say in a hoarse voice when she came in again. He wanted to tell her so much. He wanted to say that he had done nothing but think and ache for her since she had gone, that he loved her more than he thought possible, that he wanted to start over again and recapture the magical excitement between them.

"Hush." She laid her finger over his mouth. "We'll talk later." She pulled him to his feet and led him into the bathroom. The hot water in the tub had released the fragrance of the roses until the steam condensing on the mirror and sliding down the glass was pure perfume. She pulled his plaid flannel shirt out of his jeans but before unfastening it, she counted down the buttons on the front. "She loves me, she loves me not, she loves me . . ." she recited until she reached the last button on the shirt. "She loves me not."

Although it was only a child's game, Nick winced. He didn't know if he could stand it if she didn't love him. He had so much richness and privilege in life. Why couldn't he have the only thing he really wanted?

Susan gripped the front of his shirt with both hands and pulled. Buttons flew across the room like popcorn thrown into a crackling fire. "She loves me!"

A faint smile tugged at his lips. Hope flooded into his spent soul.

She continued to undress him and then herself. When they were both naked, she wrapped her arms around his neck and pulled him as close as possible. She allowed herself that luxury in a lovemaking that she intended to be all for him. She wanted to make up for her previous uncertainty and hesitation; she wanted him to know as sure as the sunrise each morning that she loved him.

A big sigh escaped her, as she pressed against his big, strong body. She could feel his warmth and miraculous life. She was happy.

Nick encircled her waist with his arms, hugging her closer still. Susan's breath tickled the hair on his chest. After days of sleepless torment, he was at peace.

Once they were in the tub, she lathered a thick cotton washcloth with soap and rubbed his body down with it. When his skin was covered with soapy foam, she discarded the washcloth and used her hands. Her fingers slipped over his glistening flesh, sensuously remembering the contours of his muscles. She knelt behind him to wash his back. He had such a beautiful back, sometimes smooth, sometimes angular, but always strong and broad. She slid closer until her breasts were pressed against his soapy skin. She reached both arms around him and, with slow circular strokes, one hand in hypnotizing counterpoint to the other, she massaged her way downward. Her hands slipped from view beneath the water. With a groan, Nick sunk back against her, unaware that he had bitten his lip and a drop of blood more red than the roses welled in the cut. When his body began to tremble on the brink of release, she stopped.

She stood up, the water streaming down and around the curves of her body like a white marble fountain. Stepping out of the tub, she quickly dried herself before stretching out a hand to him. "Come here," she asked softly.

His toes curled into the plush rug as she dried him with a towel that was so coarse and nubby that he glowed a rosy tan when she was done. He was like a snake that had sloughed off its old brittle skin and was sleek, sinuous, and vernal again. He could feel the blood rushing through his veins in a heated dance.

He went into the bedroom and lay down in the center of the bed, his eyes fixed on her as she slipped in beside him, facing him, propped on one elbow with her body molded against his side.

"I love you," she said. She caressed his face and chest; her hand moved slowly but never stopped in its restless mission to touch all of him, to stake her claim, to leave her imprint.

"I love you," she said. Her mouth followed the trail her hand had blazed along the length of his body.

"I love you," she repeated again. Words fell from her lips like diamonds and roses. She told him of her love in a crazy jumble of song, poetry and sighs that he understood perfectly and echoed back to her.

Then he took charge, moving over her and in her with the driving force of a man who had feared that he had lost everything and then discovered that victory was his after all. There was no weakness or restraint left in him; all that remained was a triumphant masculinity that took deep pleasure in possessing her.

Susan clung to him, her knees drawn up to grip his hips, riding the fury of his passion. Her breath came in shuddering gasps as she abandoned herself to the elemental sensations that swept away all intellect. She was a woman and something deep within her responded to his strength. Let him give; she would take. Let him take; she would give.

After they had exhausted themselves with their pent-up need for each other, they lay together on the big rumpled bed. Even in their exhaustion, a hand still caressed a hip, lips brushed against a cheek, a foot stroked downward on a calf.

"That was my favorite flannel shirt you destroyed in there," Nick remarked, rumpling her hair.

"As I recall, you performed a similar service on a good silk blouse of mine not too long ago. Tit for tat." Her hand slipped down his chest to his stomach and she laid a finger on his navel. "She loves me."

"You've never said that before." He spoke cautiously, as if by a misspoken word or gesture he could destroy their precious accord.

"I've loved you all along. I was just afraid to tell you so."

"Why? Didn't you trust me?"

He didn't move, but she could feel him emotionally pull away. She was going to have to tell him the whole story. "It wasn't you. I didn't trust myself. About Richard . . ." she began.

Here at last was the truth, he thought with a rush of relief and trepidation.

"For a while, I thought I was in love with him. I desperately needed to be in love to forget about death. It is unspeakable to watch a parent suffer and slowly die. I watched my father grow thinner and turn so pale that his skin was transparent, so weak that he couldn't lift his head off the pillow." Tears welled in her eyes as she told about it.

Nick held her tightly and brushed the tears on her cheeks away with his lips until she could continue.

"So I fell in love with Richard, but he didn't want me. He was never a threat to you," she said wryly. "And then I discovered that I didn't really love him after all. We're just good friends. I mean that. It's not a euphemism or a cover-up for something else."

"Why didn't you tell me this months ago?"

She looked at him. Her eyelashes were still wet with tears, but there was a tender smile on her lips. "You wanted sex and laughter. Well, so did I," she admitted.

"What we had together in bed from the very first night was wonderful. The good times seemed so simple and easy that I didn't recognize them as an expression of love. In some ways, I took love for granted or at least, I overlooked it. In other ways, I cherished what we had so much that I didn't dare risk losing it. How could I tell you about my father or Richard? Not funny, not sexy, just sad. I wanted to keep you, not drive you away."

Nick laughed out loud at that. "Sweetheart, don't worry. I don't think there is a way in heaven or hell that you could drive me away." He cupped her chin in his hand, looked into her soft green eyes, and grew serious again. "Never in my lifetime. Not even in the hereafter."

"Sometimes," she whispered, trembling in his gaze, "you overwhelm me. I never expected to have someone like you in my life. You were a total shock to me. Like a fairy godmother or an evil genius, I summoned you and you came, you with your money, your plumb bob and cordless miter box, your body, your fun and games, your eyes, your touch. You were unbelievable, larger than life. I was afraid I would be so overshadowed by you that I would simply disappear. That's why I couldn't tell you I loved you. It would have been total capitulation."

"Why can you tell me now? What's different? What happened?"

"Chicago happened. *I'm* different." She raised herself, face glowing with excitement as she remembered that she hadn't told him about the conference yet. "Oh, Nick, you should have been there! I won! I flew back early to tell you." She scrambled out of bed to dig in her suitcase for the plaque.

He watched her kneel naked on the floor by the suitcase and waited patiently to hear her story although his thoughts were not on academic success. God, she was beautiful. His eyes memorized her gently curving slender figure, her creamy skin, the soft down at the base of her spine. He drank her in and reveled in her spontaneous affirmation of him, of them. Her award couldn't possibly have been as sweet for her as "You should have been there" was for him.

She came back to bed clutching the plaque to her bare bosom. Then, with a flourish, she presented it to him. "Ta da, the George Herbert Mead Award."

"Congratulations," he said, sitting up. With his fingertip, he traced her name, which was engraved on the gold plate. "I'm very happy for you. You worked damn hard for it and deserve the recognition." He leaned over and kissed her on the cheek. "I mean it, darling. I never meant to steal you away from your work. I suppose, in a fairly adolescent way," he confessed with a sheepish grin, "I was jealous of it. It had your attention and I didn't. Not only that, it was something you shared with Richard, a bond between you that I couldn't break or duplicate. By the way, just out of idle curiosity, what did you do with him? Weren't you supposed to drive home together?"

"I'm afraid I deserted without even saying goodbye. I did leave him a note," she said, trying to assuage her guilt. She continued, "I didn't see much of him during the conference. He was too preoccupied with a sexy young graduate student from the U of M. He'll probably get her to ride home with him."

"It's okay, Susan. You don't have to explain. As long as you love me, you can be friends with anybody you want to be, woman or man." He kissed her, his lips barely brushing against hers, a soft, tender, will-o'-the-wisp kiss. "I can even rise to the occasion and feel sorry for him."

There was a certain lack of conviction in his sympathy, but Susan let the subject drop. Enough progress had been made for now. Perhaps Richard and Nick could even be friends one day. But there were other issues that could not go unspoken. "Nick, while we're clearing the air, we need to talk about tenure, too."

He stiffened. They had managed to come together before—that first passionate night, their honeymoon, the stormy winter night in her office—only to be split apart again by academic politics. Each time the split was made more painful because of the intimacy that had preceded it. *Don't do this*, he wanted to beg her. *Don't risk it.*

"I never exactly explained why I hired you under false pretenses for the Faculty Club dance." She hesitated, embarrassment tingeing her face rosy pink, before plunging on. "Fred Harrison had warned me that the tenure committee believed I was having an affair with Richard and would vote against me. Do I need to remind you that this rumor was totally untrue?" she asked with a worried eye on Nick's face. "We spent a lot of time together because . . ."

"We were just good friends," he completed teasingly. He couldn't say he was happy hearing that other people had shared his suspicions but somehow her story made sense and took some of the pressure off him. He had unknowingly come into a situation already rife with tension. No wonder she had been so sensitive about tenure.

"Molly and I decided that I should show up at Humboldt with someone else to put the rumors to rest."

"Ah, 'Pride goeth before a fall.'"

He was so quick, she thought with wonder. He automatically understood that the injury to her woman's pride had been just as significant as the threat to her career. He knew her weaknesses and insecurities as well as her strengths and accepted her as she was. Loved her as she was.

"When I think of all the rumors we ended up starting instead of finishing—" she started to laugh. "—well, it seemed like a good idea at the time."

"It was a good idea, a splendiferous idea, an ideal idea. If you hadn't thought of it, we might never have met." He relaxed and reclined back on the bed. There were going to be no more recriminations, only open and free communication.

Susan rested against him, her head close to his on the pillow. They turned toward each other, face-to-face, so the sight of the beloved was all they could see.

"Everything came together for me in Chicago. I realized that I have nothing to fear from the likes of Will Lambert or even FTP. A few months ago, I was not willing to stand up before the faculty and defend myself because I lacked the confidence. I relied on you to defend me instead. But everything is different now! I won the award and I found out that the president of the Association wants to collaborate with me on a textbook. All of a sudden, I have options. I'm not totally dependent on Humboldt for a living anymore. I'm free from it, so I can freely choose to stay. I'm not stuck anymore."

"But you could have left Humboldt at anytime. I would have supported you."

She shook her head, but instead of stopping to explain, she continued to talk. "And then there was this man . . ."

"What?" Nick rose from the pillow.

She pushed him back down again. "Tom Sexton from the University of Chicago tried to seduce me," she said, her eyes twinkling with delight.

"I'm going to have to lock you up to keep the other men away," Nick muttered, somewhat placated by the key words tried to. "Who is this libertine anyway? An old guy?"

"No, he's about your age."

"Fat and bald?"

"Gorgeous, very sexy."

"Not too bright?"

"Brilliant."

"I give up. What was wrong with him?"

"He was about as much fun as the Spanish Inquisition. He did you a tremendous service, Nick, although you might not see it. Just as the award and textbook contract freed me from Humboldt, he freed me from you."

"What does that mean?" he asked quietly.

"He gave me a choice and all of a sudden, I realized that I have options in my personal life, too. I don't have to choose you if I don't want to. We married so quickly under such strained and unusual circumstances that I was never quite sure why I was marrying you. Sometimes it felt as though it was being forced on me . . . by you, by tenure, by Humboldt. Now, at last, I am free to choose on my own, unhampered by financial or emotional dependency. I am equal to you now, Nick." Her voice was vibrant with her conviction.

"So now, what do you choose?" He dared to ask because, in his heart, he finally knew her answer.

"You, of course." She kissed him then, long and deep. When she broke away, she whispered, "I'm sorry it took me so long."

"It was worth the wait," he replied and meant it.

"I was so scared that I was too late. I didn't know if you were going to be here when I got home. I kept calling and you weren't here. Why did you come back, Nick?"

"'Susie Q'," he replied. "I came back because that's the way you signed your note. Did I ever tell you what the Q stands for?"

"Yes, you did and very unflattering it was, too."

"Well, it's changed since then. The Q now stands for quintessential. Quintessential: of the quintessence, purest, most perfect." He held out his hand. "Pleased to meet you, Dr. Susie Quintessential Harkness Taurage."

"Ditto, Dr. Feelgood," she replied, shaking his hand.

They grinned in perfect happiness, but as they looked at each other, their laughter was displaced by desire that swept through them hot and fast.

Nick felt overwhelmed. How he loved her. And how he wanted her. Now. Immediately. No kisses or caresses, no tantalizing seduction, no whispered games. He forced himself to think of her. She would need more time. Slow down. Slow down.

"Nick!" She pushed him back against the pillows with some violence. "Q is also for quick," she said as she leaned over him. Their bodies meshed together and within minutes, they cried out as one.

Susan collapsed on his chest and lay there, listening to her heart beat with his. Eventually she gathered up enough courage to raise her head and cautiously looked at him. She had never ever responded like that before. So wild and aggressive.

His brown eyes were alight with mischief, making the gold flecks more pronounced, and his lips were curved into a cat-that-ate-the-canary smile. "'To love her,'" he observed with great satisfaction, "'was a liberal education.'"

HARLEQUIN
American Romance®

THE ROMANCE THAT STARTED IT ALL!

For Diane Bauer and Nick Granatelli, the walk down the aisle
was a rocky road....

Don't miss the romantic prequel to WITH THIS RING—

I THEE WED
BY ANNE McALLISTER

Harlequin American Romance #387

Let Anne McAllister take you to Cambridge, Massachusetts, to
the night when an innocent blind date brought a reluctant Diane
Bauer and Nick Granatelli together. For Diane, a smoldering
attraction like theirs had only one fate, one future—marriage.
The hard part, she learned, was convincing her intended....

Watch for Anne McAllister's I THEE WED, available *now* from
Harlequin American Romance.

ITW

You'll flip . . . your pages won't!
Read paperbacks *hands-free* with

Book Mate • I

The perfect "mate" for all your romance paperbacks

**Traveling • Vacationing • At Work • In Bed • Studying
• Cooking • Eating**

Perfect size for all standard paperbacks, this wonderful invention makes reading a pure pleasure! Ingenious design holds paperback books OPEN and FLAT so even wind can't ruffle pages — leaves your hands free to do other things. Reinforced, wipe-clean vinyl-covered holder flexes to let you turn pages without undoing the strap . . . supports paperbacks so well, they have the strength of hardcovers!

Pages turn WITHOUT opening the strap.

SEE-THROUGH STRAP

Reinforced back stays flat.

Built in bookmark

BOOK MARK

BACK COVER HOLDING STRIP

10" x 7¼", opened.
Snaps closed for easy carrying, too